The BOOB Girls V

The **B**urned **O**ut **O**ld **B**roads at Table 12

The Secret Of The Red Cane

A Novel by Joy Johnson

Copyright ©2013 Joy Johnson

ISBN: 1-56123-243-7

Library of Congress information on file.

CENTERING CORPORATION
AND
GRIEF DIGEST MAGAZINE
GRIEF RESOURCES

Order from: www.centering.org
1-866-218-0101 or 1-402-553-1200
centeringcorp@aol.com

GRIEF ILLUSTRATED PRESS

Dedicated to all of us who grew up with Nancy Drew

Nancy is 80 years old now.
She is now and has always been, one of us.

Part One

Seasoned Nancy Drews

Nancy Drew: "I wonder who tried to kill us."
Corky: "Yeah, I'm wondering that too. In fact, I'm kind of freaking out about it!"

Nancy Drew: "If you shoot me, that'll leave all kinds of evidence. Really messy."
(thug prepares to strangle her)

Nancy Drew: "Strangulation leaves a traceable handprint."

Hadley Joy Morris-Whitfield: *We all grew up with Nancy Drew.*

Marge Aaron: *She inspired me to go into police work, that's for sure.*

Mary Rose McGill: *She had so many exclamation points!*

Robinson Leary: *She was so good she could have been black. Today at least, one or two of her friends would be black.*

Mirror, Mirror: It's Heavy Duty
Being Such A Beauty!

The reflection smiled back.

"You are so beautiful," the woman looking into the mirror said. The reflection smiled more.

"I do declare, I love my hair." The reflection patted its hair.

"I hate to be crass, but get a load of this ass!"

The refection turned sideways and looked at its rear.

"And everything in its place, that is such a nice face!" The reflection pursed its lips to return a kiss.

"Admire the rest, but just look at that chest," she said. The reflection put its hands on its hips, tilted its head and stuck out its chest. It turned, bent over just a little and patted its rear end. The woman smoothed her slacks over her hips.

"They're right. No panty line," she muttered. She straightened up and looked into the mirror one last time. She smiled. She turned. The reflection's back appeared as the woman switched off the bathroom light and walked out her front door to meet her friends at table 12 in the Meadow Lakes dining room. She forced another smile.

Mary Rose McGill had just put on her first pair of Depends super absorbent underwear for those slightly or embarrassingly incontinent, and she was determined to maintain a good attitude.

Hadley Joy Morris-Whitfield, Dr. Robinson Leary and Marge Aaron lifted their coffee cups to her as she approached table 12.

"Let's see it," Hadley said.

"Bend over, girl," Robbie Leary added.

Marge Aaron smiled. "The make-up is perfect, the outfit designer-worthy. You look beautiful, Mary Rose."

Mary Rose turned her back to them and bent over.

"No panty line at all," Hadley said. Then she grinned and sang, "I'll get *by* with a little help from Depends."

"No bulge, either," Marge added and made a face at Hadley.

"But how do they feel, Mary Rose," Robbie asked. "That's the big question."

Mary Rose McGill dropped into her seat. "The Depends feel okay. And I gave myself a pep talk and did the 'I am beautiful' thing, but I still just hate it. I hate leaking. I hate having to run to the bathroom and half the time not making it. *I just hate being old!*" She grabbed the coffee pot in the middle of the table and poured herself a cup of decaf. "At least when you three tell me I look great you don't add, *'for your age.'* I've actually had someone say that to me."

"Like the song says," Hadley added, "no one sends us roses anymore. And no one just says, 'You're pretty.' We always, 'look nice.'"

"For our age." Marge Aaron added, then laughed.

They were four retired widows, best friends, confidantes and four-women support group. They were family. They were the **B**urned **O**ut **O**ld **B**roads at Table 12.

Hadley Joy Morris-Whitfield was tall with short white hair that was thick and bouncy. She, like most older women, had thickened some as she grew older. She liked coordinated pantsuits, tweeds and Channel perfume. Her husband had died in a fiery private plane crash in the mountains, and her only child, David, was an attorney in Omaha. Hadley had style and money. Hadley had one of the big third-floor, three bedroom apartments in Meadow Lakes Retirement Community, and that's where the girls went for movie marathons, holiday or birthday dinners, and to generally, as her grandchildren loved to say, "chill and hang out."

Hadley also had an on-going, long-distance relationship with Wes Longbow, a retired sheriff on the west coast. Wes was the most handsome Native American man Hadley could imagine. He was literally tall, dark and handsome and together they made a striking couple. Wes looked trim and fit in western suits and cowboy boots. Trouble was, Hadley wasn't going to leave her family in Omaha, Nebraska, a place she dearly loved, and Wes didn't want to leave the west coast where he had lived his entire life. They got together for some holidays, an occasional week-long vacation and at times when they just simply needed each other. "We get along great," Hadley had said more than once. "We don't see each other often enough to disagree about anything."

The truth was, Hadley didn't want to leave her three friends, whose mission today was to enforce Mary Rose McGill's knowledge that she was physically beautiful whether or not she wore Depends underwear. They were doing so at table 12 in the dining room, their breakfast plates before them, coffee steaming from their white porcelain cups, scrambled eggs and bacon and hot muffins smelling a lot like Heaven.

Four years ago another woman, who had once sat where Marge Aaron now parked her sizeable rear, had named them The BOOB Girls: The Burned Out Old Broads at Table 12. Maggie Patten, a rough, tough, retired rancher from Nebraska's Sand Hills, had shot five bullets into her mean-spirited, mean-talking, just plain mean husband's gravestone and taken the girls – with no forwarding address – on a trip west that had changed their lives. Especially when their Maggie had died on a short cruise and they had weighted her body down with her suitcase and thrown her overboard for a secret and slightly illegal burial at sea.

That kind of thing gives women a rather strong bond.

Hadley turned toward Mary Rose, "Remember my four words I said over and over when I had uterine cancer? *Grace, Humor, Courage and Confidence.*"

Mary Rose nodded. "Good words."

They were quiet for a minute, then Robinson Leary looked up at Hadley. "Hah!" She said. "I remember other words from your cancer story. I remember how when you were on the wonderful table in the doc's office, with your feet in the stirrups, your super-cute OB-GYN pulled out the biopsy tube and said, 'Fantastic!' because it looked good. And you said," Robbie pointed her fork at Hadley, "Do you know what it means to a lady my age to have a handsome young man look between her legs and say, 'fantastic?'"

Hadley grinned and her eyes twinkled. "You have your own stories, Dr. Leary. I remember how, when your husband died in his sleep, before you called anyone you showered, dressed and went to the bank. If I remember right, you went up to the teller and said you wanted to get into your safety deposit box and the teller said, 'Sure, Dr. Leary, where's that professor husband of yours?' and you said...." She grinned and looked at Robbie who smiled a broad smile.

"He's still in bed," Robbie said. "I was worried about the law closing the safety deposit box until probate." She shrugged and took a healthy bite of her blueberry muffin.

"Widows, even new ones, are resourceful," Marge Aaron nodded toward Robbie and took a sip of her coffee. She looked at Hadley. "I like *Grace, Humor, Courage and Confidence,* Hadley. As for me, when my husband was so sick I used STDs."

Robbie's eyebrows raised and Mary Rose's eyes got wide. "Sexually Transmitted Diseases?" Robbie asked with a smile.

"Nope," Marge replied. *"Strong, Tough, Determined and Smart.* Saying those words over and over through the day got me through the hell that surrounded us."

"Your 'T' could stand for *Tender*, too, Marge. You're as tender as you are tough."

They all looked at Marge and smiled.

"I still resolve to find something good in every day and live a life of gratitude," Robbie said.

"Okay! Okay!" Mary Rose grinned and looked at her friends. "I'm okay wearing Depends. Will you three stop being so damn helpful?"

Robbie bopped her on the arm and grinned. "Not on your life, girlfriend! You're way too much fun."

Robinson Leary was half black, half Cajun with salt and pepper hair and skin the color of a fine latte. Her husband, a long-time multiple sclerosis patient, had been wheelchair bound and the love of her life. They had both taught at Creighton University and lived in the trendy Mayfair Building in Omaha's even trendier Old Market. Robinson Leary liked to combine blacks and whites from her wardrobe, and because she and her husband were basketball fans, Robbie had more than one Creighton Bluejays workout suit and even more Bluejays jackets.

Marge Aaron spoke up. "I'm still thinking about you, Mary Rose. Doing something like wearing your first pair of Depends is kind of a rite of passage, a rite into doing something you need to do because you've changed and something you do even though you don't like doing it. It grows your soul in some strange way. It's like a grown child's first dinner for their parents in that child's own apartment."

Marge Aaron was a retired homicide detective. She was big, boisterous and super alert. She saw things others didn't see; she was bigger than life and almost as tall as Hadley. Marge Aaron knew how to fight and she had a gun. In fact, she had more than a gun. She had a Red Cane which she always carried over her arm. It was a beautiful cane, outfitted with five colorful jewels that stood out against the apple bright background.

Press one jewel and the cane turned into a taser.

Press another jewel and the cane became a low-powered rifle.

A third jewel released tripping pellets all over the floor.

A fourth jewel created a red smoke screen and the fifth jewel popped out two knives, ready to be grabbed and put to use.

The Red Cane also had a golden lariat in the handle. Just like *Wonder Woman's*.

Marge did not resemble *Wonder Woman* the Amazon, though she was an amazon in her own right. She was large, in the way some women were meant to be large. Her gray hair still had strands of mouse brown in it and was thin and curly in a minimum-maintenance sort of way. Like Hadley, she wore pantsuits, always in a dark color, and her shoes were horridly practical.

Marge's husband was also a cop, as was her son. A daughter was FBI. Marge had married law enforcement and given birth to law enforcement. She had seen her share of death and suffering. One long-term suffering and hard death had belonged to her husband, the only one of the girls' husbands to have had such an ending. It had led Marge to firmly believe that it is often more difficult to *see* suffering than to *be* suffering. Life could be hard, and Marge Aaron had seen some of the worst of it.

She looked across the table at Mary Rose. The sun through the floor-to-ceiling window in the dining room hit the top of their table and turned their juice glasses into a mini-rainbow of orange, grape, cranberry and tomato. "I always loved what you say about older women being beautiful, Mary Rose. Lay it on us, girl. Say it for us."

Mary Rose folded her napkin and put it beside her plate. She smiled, looked at her friends and said, "Older women are beautiful! Just look at our faces. Our faces are chiseled and sculpted by tears and laughter, joy and sorrow. Our hair is blown thin by winds of experience.

And there is so much knowledge and wisdom in our heads, our heads can't hold it all. It has to trickle down into the rest of our bodies and that's why we get thicker as we age." They were quiet for a moment, looking at Mary Rose.

Mary Rose McGill had been a surprise at table 12. When she first arrived, she was sad, angry and dowdy to the max. She had fourteen housedresses, two pairs of clunky, ugly shoes, was sixty pounds overweight and depressed. Her four daughters had simply up and moved her into Meadow Lakes Retirement Community after her husband died following a massive stroke while attending his daily mass. She had no say about it. She hated it. But after she was assigned, along with the other three, to eat together at table 12, she changed. She changed thanks to the love and friendship of other women who saw her as she could be.

Women have a friendship unlike that of men. Being the ancient purveyors of language and the bearers of children, we learned centuries ago to talk to each other. We learned to see each other both as we are and as we can be. Studies show that the more friends a woman has, the healthier she is, even when the ills of old age come calling; and let's face it, old age tends to come at a really bad time.

When men are stressed, they tend to go off by themselves and work. When women are stressed, they tend to clean, make coffee and call a girlfriend. At table 12 Mary Rose McGill learned all about women's friendship. She was accepted as she was, she was seen as what she could be, and she became that vision. Mary Rose McGill lost sixty pounds. She got a new wardrobe – featuring a good deal of pink – and she got new glasses with red frames. Mary Rose McGill dyed her hair blonde. She was almost to the point of writing those four daughters, who had pulled up with a U-Haul and moved her from her home to this place, a long thank you letter.

"You know what is kind of nice," she told the girls. "These Depends actually look a lot like real panties. They even have the sides cut up high like the expensive briefs."

"Did somebody say, 'panties and briefs?'" Wiley Vondra stood behind Mary Rose's chair and leaned on it.

"Yo, Wiley," the girls said together.

He pulled up a chair from a neighboring table and sat down. "What's up, ladies?"
Mary Rose patted Wiley's shoulder. "I put on my first pair of Depends underwear this morning," she said. "I hate it but I needed to do it."

"Growin' old sucks," Wiley said to the table in general.

Wiley Vondra was the naked man in the laundry room. On the fifteenth of every month, at midnight he could be found in the laundry room wearing only his cowboy boots, brown leather vest and old Stetson. When Wiley Vondra did his laundry, he did *all* his laundry. He was also Mary Rose's main squeeze. He lifted her face toward his and kissed her forehead. Wiley was tall, thin and had just grown his hair out into a ponytail. He looked like an aging hippie with a country western attitude. He looked at the girls over rimless bifocals. His eyes creased as he grinned. "Alphonso's on his way over."

Alphonso Greatwood's scooter, The Mean Machine, glided up beside table 12. He reached over to the next table, lifted a chair up and over his head, and set it between Marge and Robbie. Marge raised her eyebrows and looked at Robbie. Those chairs were heavy and Alphonso had made it look like a pickup stick. He climbed off his Mean Machine and sat in the chair. "Ladies," he said and he smiled at Robbie then Marge.

Alphonso Greatwood was famous and rich. He had played pro-football for years for the Kansas City Chiefs and had been Pro-Bowl MVP, getting so many hits on his helmet that sometimes his words didn't come out right. But, much like Mary Rose, once he had found friends who didn't much care how he sounded or looked or how many old endorsements he had, his words had cleared up a lot and he was grateful. Big, black, still strong, Alphonso had an attractive look, a totally bald head and thighs that made watermelons envious. He had fallen in love with Robinson Leary, but Robinson Leary wasn't ready for a commitment and, deep in her heart, wasn't sure she wanted to be involved with another man with multiple disabilities.

For one thing, Alphonso's knees were shot beyond repair, he had a neck injury (Peyton

Manning was a piker), and his back had been fractured twice. He had a van equipped so he could drive it and he had his Mean Machine. The Mean Machine was green now, having had a new paint job the autumn before. It had racing stripes, a roll bar, a GPS on the handlebars and a seat behind the driver's with "Bitch Seat" in orange letters. When Alphonso went forward in The Mean Machine, he pushed a button that played the theme from *Happy Days* because he was the original "Fonz." When he backed up, another button played the Nebraska fight song. Alphonso had never liked the Chief's musical selections. He loved his Mean Machine. He loved being a traffic hazard in a retirement community.

"Gossip!" Alphonso said. "I just came from the manager's office. John says Meadow Lakes has just been sold to a group from Florida, The Busch Family, Inc." They stared at him. Hadley stood up, grabbed two clean cups from another table and signaled a server to bring two fresh pots of coffee: one regular, one decaf.

"I have a sign in my kitchen that says, 'Will trade coffee for gossip.'" Hadley said. "And I just ordered two new pots of java. Speak, great black one."

Alphonso chuckled. "All John knew was that they own a lot of properties and they run the places themselves when they first buy them. There are two brothers and two sisters who will be showing up any time now." He shrugged. "Frankly, I don't give a rat's hiney as long as they keep the place clean and the food hot." He reached over and patted Marge's knee. She laughed and made a show of swatting his hand away. Robbie did an eye roll.

Alphonso pulled a sheet of paper out of his back pocket. "I saved these just for you." He winked and smiled at Robbie, then turned and grinned at Marge. "They're ads that were in a London newspaper." He pulled reading glasses out of his shirt pocket, put them on and peered over his big nose. He began to read: "FREE YORKSHIRE TERRIER. 8 years old. Hateful little bastard. Bites!" He looked around the table and saw the smiles he expected. He read on: "FREE PUPPIES - 1/2 Cocker Spaniel, 1/2 sneaky neighbor's dog." Wiley laughed out loud. "FREE PUPPIES. Mother is a Kennel Club registered German Shepherd. Father is a Super Dog, able to leap tall fences in a single bound."

"I wish my mind was that warped and I could think like that," Marge said.

"There's one more," Alphonso smiled. "COWS, CALVES: NEVER BRED. Also 1 gay bull for sale." He pocketed his glasses, smiled at his success in not screwing up a single word.

The table was covered with the warm, comfortable banter of good friends, laughter and people talking to each other at the same time. It was all punctuated by the soft clink of coffee cups on saucers and coffee being poured.

Alphonso leaned into the table and said, "What pisses me off is now that I have my head together, my body is falling apart." He laughed and looked up. "Getting crowded here. I see the Hosemoffs coming toward us."

Gertrude and Heathcliff Hosemoff were a sweet couple. Of medium height, they had been married for seventy years. Back in those days, people married young and the Hosemoffs had tied the knot on Gertrude's fifteenth birthday. At Meadow Lakes Retirement Community, they were sometimes called WCC: World's Cutest Couple. For five years running, they had been voted Valentine King and Queen.

Gertrude looked like a little Mother Goose with white curls, wire-rimmed glasses, and a soft, slightly pudgy body. Heathcliff was two inches taller, skinny as Jack Sprat and still obviously smitten with his lady love.

Wiley got up from his chair, moved behind Alphonso and sat in the Bitch Seat on The Mean Machine, making a gesture to Gertrude to take his chair.

"Thank you, Wiley, but I'll just stand," Gertrude said.

"We won't be here long," Heathcliff finished.

"Nice walking stick there, Heathcliff,"

Alphonso said, pointing to the carved wooden cane upon which Heathcliff Hosemoff was leaning heavily.

"It's a great cane," Heathcliff said.

"He calls it 'John M'Cane," Gertrude giggled.

Hadley smiled. "Did you name your cane too, Gertrude?"

"She did indeed," Heathcliff pointed to the pink cane covered with flowers that was getting an equally heavy lean from his wife.

Gertrude held up the cane for them to see. "I call it Nova."

"Nova Cane," Robbie and Mary Rose said together.

The old couple looked at everyone crowded around table 12, nodded, then settled their gaze on Marge Aaron.

"Marge," Gertrude began. "We've met you a few times…"

"Not enough to really get to know you, but…" Heathcliff said.

"Enough to get a feel for the way you like to help people…" Gertrude added.

"Who need desperate assistance," Heathcliff finished.

"We are in need of such assistance."

"And we understand you were once a detective and you have…"

"a gun. Maybe more than one." They were experts at finishing each other's sentences.

Marge looked surprised, blinked and gave a little shrug. "What do you need, folks? Especially, what do you need that would involve a firearm?"

Heathcliff put his arm around Gertrude's shoulder. "We have been together for seventy years."

"We are still in love, not just loving each other," Gertrude added.

"In Love." Heathcliff said. "Do you realize how few people can say that?"

Everyone looked at them.

"We don't want one of us to die, leaving the other helpless and…" Gertrude sighed.

"Mired in grief," Heathcliff finished.

"I don't see how I can help," Marge said. "I do know a few bereavement counselors to help whichever one of you survives."

"That's not what we want," Gertrude said.

"We want to die together," Heathcliff added. They looked intently at Marge.

"We want you to kill us," they said together.

Quiet, Good Times –
Precious and All Too Brief

"So you refused to off the Hosemoffs," Mary Rose said to Marge.

"What were they thinking?" Marge said. "Am I supposed to be a cane-wielding killer in clunky shoes?"

"Shoes may be bad, but your hair is good," Hadley smiled.

They were seated at a table in their favorite coffee shop, The Village Grinder. The Grinder was attached to their favorite bookstore, The

Bookworm. Robbie had wanted to find a children's book with her favorite poem and to pick up a book or two of Nancy Drew mysteries before they had their next movie marathon, which would consist of three old Nancy Drew movies.

"I can understand them wanting to die together," Robbie said, turning her oversized green coffee cup around and around on their little table. "My husband and I used to talk about wishing we could die together. Then that movie came out, *The Notebook*, and James Garner climbed into bed with his wife, who had terrible Alzheimer's, and she said, 'Do you think our love is strong enough?' and he said, 'I think our love can do anything it wants to do,' and they died in each other's arms." She was talking very fast and looked as if she was going to cry. "Well, our love was strong, too, and the Hosemoffs probably take the cake for loving each other, so why can't they just lie down and die together?"

She looked up at them and they all looked back at her with tender eyes. "One thing for sure, Robinson Leary," Mary Rose said, touching Robbie's arm. "I'm damned glad you and your husband *didn't* die together. I don't know what I would do without you, girlfriend." The others nodded vigorously and Marge blew her nose on her little paper napkin. They smiled at each other and went back to talking about what snacks they wanted for their Nancy Drew movie marathon.

No one had shown up yet to claim ownership of Meadow Lakes Retirement Community and they had had a good week. Mary Rose had worked at her church's rummage sale and pulled, shoved and bribed Hadley, Robbie and Marge into helping. Coffee today was on her. Hadley had enjoyed a long lunch at Mark's Bistro in Dundee with friends from her high school class who were passing through town. Robbie had gotten involved with a book club called Guilty Pleasures and was enjoying mysteries with a good group. And Marge had gotten a call from a sister-in-law from Chicago who was passing through Omaha. They were going to spend time in the Old Market and maybe take in a movie.

They finished their coffees, said goodbye to Patty, the owner of Village Grinder, wandered through The Bookworm one last time, saying goodbye and getting hugs from the ladies who worked there, and climbed into their black Hummer, a leftover from Maggie Patten days.

"Anybody for a game of monopoly when we get back?" Hadley asked. A granddaughter had given her a new monopoly game for Christmas and they had yet to test drive it.

"I wish we could create a Nancy Drew Monopoly game," Robbie said. "We probably couldn't find enough locations, but the pieces could be fun: an old clock, a little staircase, a Loch Ness monster, a spyglass, a little magnifying glass, her hat, her old car." She became lost in deep thoughts of other game pieces as Hadley rolled the big vehicle out of The Bookworm parking lot.

There's A Pirate Climbin' in the Winda

They set up the Monopoly board on table 12 right after breakfast the next day. Robbie had a stack of children's books beside her and was leafing through each one as Mary Rose claimed the right to be banker. Wiley Vondra came by with a new pot of decaf and four clean mugs, ready to see them settle in for a game that would probably last until lunchtime.

"Drat!" Robbie said, shaking her head and dropping the book she was holding on top of the stack beside her chair. "I can't find it!"
"What are you looking for?" Wiley asked.
"A great children's poem. If I could remember the author I could find it online, but I've Googled and Googled and nothing comes up. It's a fun poem about a dog named Mustard, a cat named Ink and a girl named Belinda who looks up and sees a pirate climbin' through the winda. It was a feminist little poem by a man and I loved it, and like an idiot I didn't buy the book it was in. Drat! Drat! Drat!"

Wiley grinned. "That's what you four need: A Py-rate climbin' in the winda. That fits you a lot better than trying to be the first to get a hotel on Marvin Gardens." He sat the mugs down beside each girl and poured them coffee. "You need your very own Py-rate." He chuckled.

"Thanks Wiley," they all said together and Marge Aaron rolled the dice to start the game.

Hadley had just put a house on Park Place when Robbie yelled, "I found it, I found it, I found it!"

They stopped playing and waited. Robbie opened up a book of poetry for children. It was big and had a cover with all the colors of the rainbow. "It was by Ogden Nash in 1936," she said. "And I couldn't remember the title, but it's *The Tale of Custard the Dragon.*" She cleared her throat. "It's about a cowardly dragon who ate the pirate comin' in the winda." She read the poem aloud, and just after she read the part that said:

"Suddenly, suddenly they heard a nasty sound, And Mustard growled, and they all looked around.

Meowch! cried Ink, and Ooh! cried Belinda, For there was a pirate, climbing in the winda."

Mary Rose reached over, just as suddenly, and grabbed Robbie's arm. "Oh for Heaven's sake!" she said, and she pointed to the small window next to the door that led outside to the patio. "Look what Wiley and Alphonso have done now!"

They turned and looked. There, trying to open the window was a dark-skinned man dressed in a poncho, cowboy boots and a big Mexican sombrero. He was struggling with the window, trying to force it open. He bent and laid something on the ground, pushed up with all his might and the window slowly groaned and started even more slowly to open.

"Should we tell him the door next to that window is never locked?" Robbie asked.

"Naw," Marge said.

"Why spoil his fun?" Hadley asked.

"It's good exercise for him," Mary Rose added.

They watched. The man, of medium height, had a handlebar mustache and little goatee. He was trying to wrestle something off the ground and get one leg through the window at the same time. He finally rolled through the window and knelt down on the dining room floor, picking something up in each hand.

"Wiley and Alphonso have out-done themselves getting us a real pirate," Mary Rose said. She squinted at the man. "Well, at least a sort-of pirate."

"I don't recognize him as one of the guys who live here," Robbie said, "But with that hat and mustache, it's hard to tell." She turned her chair so she could see better. After about two minutes of catching his breath and gathering up whatever he was gathering up, the man stood with some effort and turned toward the four girls at table 12. He jumped. He looked as if he hadn't known they were there.

"Nice touch," Marge said.

"Should we applaud now?" Mary Rose asked.

"I don't think so," Marge said. Her voice had a strange edge to it. Then, like Marge, they all really looked at the pirate who had just climbed through their winda.

A massive ammunition belt was draped from one shoulder to his opposite hip. In one hand he held what looked like a grenade, in the other was a pistol, and there was a mean-looking knife he held tight in his teeth. His sombrero had slipped down over his eyes. He pushed it up with the fist that held the grenade.

"Bit overdone," Hadley said.

"But cute," Mary Rose nodded.

Robbie leaned forward over the table as if that would give her a closer view. "I still don't recognize him, and Wiley and Alphonso couldn't have gotten some actor from the outside in just an hour or two. He has to be a resident."

Marge still didn't say anything.

The strange man walked toward them with big, strong steps. He stopped in front of the table.

"Ma cramme diss sloppery im da mame of Bursch!"

Mary Rose smiled. "Honey, we can't understand a word you're saying. Now hand me that grenade and take the knife out of your mouth." She was using her "mother voice." She held out her hand like a kindergarten teacher would for a student's gum.

The man stared at her and looked shocked. Instead of handing her the grenade, he lifted the pistol to point at Mary Rose. At the same time, Marge lifted her cane, pressed a jewel and tasered him in the balls. He went down, the knife clattering out of his mouth, the grenade rolling under the table and the pistol sliding toward Marge, who calmly and quickly picked it up.

"Marge!" the other three girls yelled at the same time and jumped to their feet. Robbie's chair fell over with a bang, Mary Rose knocked the Monopoly bank money onto the board and Hadley's mug hopped three times as if it were trying to escape. They rushed over to the prone man and looked down at him.

"You tasered our pirate!" Hadley said.

"In his manly parts!" Robbie added.

"He's dressed so cute, too," Mary Rose almost whined.

The Mexican pirate stirred and tried to roll over. Marge tasered him again, in the same place.

He lay still.

"Help me lean him up against the wall," Marge said. "They'll be coming in to set up for lunch pretty soon and I don't think we want to be here. He may not remember us when he wakes up…if we're lucky."

They grunted, pulled and dragged the prone pirate to a nearby corner of the dining room, Marge put her arms under his and propped him up against the wall, his legs spread apart, his hat over his eyes. He looked for all the world as if it was siesta time south of the border.

They gathered up the Monopoly set in record time. "I won, by the way," Hadley said. Then Marge picked up the grenade, laid it on the pirates lap and led the way out of the dining room as fast as she could go, the Red Cane over her arm and hitting her hip now and then as she tried to walk even faster. She had tucked the pistol into the back of her slacks. She herded them all into the elevator and pressed the button for the third floor and Hadley's apartment.

Hadley's apartment breathed contentment, comfort and peace. Done in mauves and whites with a touch of bright blue, it was perfect for their dinners and movies. They took seats in the living room and everyone looked at Marge Aaron.

"Marge, talk to us," Hadley said.

"He was no hired pirate recruited by Alphonso and Wiley," Marge said. "That gun, the ammo, the grenade were all real. And if I'm not wrong, he's Huckleberry Busch, also known as "Whacker." He's the Busch family enforcer, but he's been clever enough to never get convicted. He's about our age and I remember all the notices about him that came through homicide when I was there. If this is the wicked Busch family from Florida who just bought Meadow Lakes, we're in for some trouble."

An uneasy silence settled over the room. Robbie held her stack of books tightly on her lap, Mary Rose clutched the Monopoly set and Hadley still had four mugs that belonged in the dining room in her hands. Marge had only the pirate's pistol and her Red Cane, which rested harmless and quiet in her lap.

They ate quickly-made sandwiches in Hadley's apartment and avoided the Meadow Lakes dining room or being seen anywhere for that matter. After the sandwiches had all been eaten, they decided on an afternoon of movies.

They had already had movie marathons a few times this year. Marathons included a full afternoon and early evening of movies, popcorn mixed with goldfish crackers and M&Ms, along with cheap champagne. Most of the time, by early evening one or all of the movie watchers was sound asleep on the couch or in her chair.

This year had featured movies by Marge's favorite, Dame Judi Dench, as "M" in the James Bond movies. Hadley had chosen *Guess Who's Coming to Dinner, On Golden Pond* and *Lion in Winter* because she loved Katharine Hepburn. After the last movie Hadley had said, "I love that line where she holds up the crown jewels and says, 'I'd hang you from the nipples, but they would shock the children.' Think how much fun it would be to do something that would shock your children."

Mary Rose had gotten three old Nancy Drew movies and she selected one of them for the afternoon viewing.

"I loved her hat and dresses," Mary Rose said when *Nancy Drew: Detective* was rolling up the credits on Hadley's big screen TV. "Never slacks, always dresses, and neat little shoes, no sneakers."

"It was 1938, for Pete's sake," Robbie countered. "We didn't start wearing slacks until the 1950's. And," she grinned and looked around at them, "did you guys ever put on your jeans and get in the bathtub and soak 'em good then let them dry on you?"
Hadley laughed. "I did."

"You know," Marge said, "It was really quite a feminist little movie. Nancy did most of the driving in that old car."

"It had a crank to start it!" Mary Rose giggled. "And when her dad said, 'Turn this car around and go home, Nancy, this is getting too dangerous for you,' how many fathers and husbands think they know better than women and try to get them back into the safety of the kitchen?"

"A kitchen where your stove could explode," Robbie added. "Then boyfriend Ted tells her she's just like all women and he can't convince her of anything."

"Men," Hadley said and did an eye roll.

Blooming Busches

They all met the next morning at table 12, after having eaten all of Hadley's microwave popcorn supply while watching the movie and cleaning out all her lunchmeat for dinner sandwiches. The dining room was quiet with morning sun streaming in through the floor-to-ceiling windows. There were no pirates leaning against the wall, no knives except those placed neatly on the napkins beside the china plates. Pleasant odors of bacon, eggs and ham filled the room and blended in with the sunshine.

"Looks good so far," Marge said as they sat their plates down after going through the ample buffet. They settled into their chairs and put their napkins on their laps. That's when the door from the kitchen opened and four people walked through into the dining room. The last one through the door was their pirate, who sneered his way to a spot near the buffet. The man leading the group was also leading an oversized Bull Mastiff, easily the biggest dog any of the girls had ever seen. The dog was brown with a huge black muzzle.

"He's bigger than a St. Bernard!" Robbie whispered.

"He's as big as a small horse!" Hadley added.

"He's like that two-headed dog in the Harry Potter movie," Marge said.

The dog sat, looked around the dining room, began to stare at Mary Rose and started to drool.

"He's looking at me like I have something to eat," Mary Rose said, sliding her chair closer to Marge.

"He's looking at you like you ARE something to eat!" Marge whispered back.

The man with the dog reached over and tapped a spoon on the buffet table to demand silence. It wasn't necessary. It was already so quiet you could hear a pin drop. Instead, the room was filled with the heavy panting sounds of the giant dog.

"Ladies and gentlemen, I am Thornton Busch, better known as 'Thorny.'" He was about six feet tall, wore a three-piece suit, expensive tie, black shiny shoes with spats, and a pocket watch, fob and chain hung from a pocket on his vest. He had dyed black hair that was thinning dramatically and a small mustache that made him look like the little groom on a wedding cake. The big dog sat obediently by his side, its head rising above the man's waist. It was still staring at Mary Rose and the pirate was staring at all four of them.

The man patted the mastiff's head. "This is Geoffrey." The dog didn't move. "Since mastiffs were bred to protect large estates in Great Britain, his name has the British spelling, with a 'G.' Geoffrey, say hello to your new friends, our residents." The dog growled a low, mean growl.

"You can all feel safer now," Thorny said with a tight little smile. "Geoffrey will be protecting you. We have just let our security team go so they can find better jobs and spend more time with their families. We all love family values, don't we." It wasn't a question.

"Let security go," Marge whispered under her breath.

"Let me introduce your new concierge, my sister, Lilac Busch." Lilac stepped beside Thorny and did a little finger wave. Her hair was dyed as blonde as her brother's was dyed black. She too was tall, probably five feet eight inches and a size 2. Skinny little legs showed from beneath her mini-skirt, which was black and perfectly matching her Chanel top with the big double "C" logo made up of sequins. She wore four-inch black heels and her fingers had long nails that sported a French manicure. Geoffrey kept on drooling and looking at Mary Rose McGill.

"And now," Thorny Busch said, "Your new CFO – that stands for Chief Financial Officer."

"We know what it means!" Hadley said out loud. People at tables near table 12 looked over, grinned and nodded.

"Chief Financial Officer –" Thorny continued as if nothing had happened. "Please welcome my sister Rose." He started a round of applause, which was less than he had hoped for.

"Rose Busch?" Robbie whispered. "Who named these people?"

Rose was plump and while we used to call ladies slightly overweight, "pleasingly plump," this was not the case with this Ms. Busch. She was at least three inches shorter than her sister, her hair was straight and stopped suddenly just below her ears, showing off its mouse-brown-mixed-with-gray lack of life and color. She wore a baggy brown dress and running shoes with what looked like support hose. Her glasses looked too big for her face and had thick brown rims to hold the thick foggy-looking lenses.

"OMG," Mary Rose whispered to Marge, "she actually has a pencil behind her ear!"

Marge nodded and cradled her Red Cane in her lap.

"And lastly," Thorny announced, "our beloved brother, Huckleberry, also known as 'Whacker' Busch. He's our general building manager and grounds supervisor. He's our handy man and will take care of all our problems here at Meadow Lakes Retirement Community. Now enjoy your breakfast and, if you have any questions, we'll be in our offices. Oh, and dear Lilac will also take the place of Jane, your fine activities director who has gone on an extended vacation."

"There goes the Bingo games," Robbie grinned.

"No more Wii bowling." Hadley added.

"Maybe Whacker will provide us with knife throwing and target practice," Marge said.

"I really don't like that dog," Mary Rose said. Geoffrey was following his owner out of the dining room, but his big head was still turned toward Mary Rose. Whacker Busch's big head was also turned their way, so much so that he nearly banged into the wall on his way out the door.

Here Chick, Chick, Chick

Things were wonderfully normal for a few days. There was a soft spring shower that gave everything a newly-washed look and smell. Hadley won two more Monopoly games and the Busches and Geoffrey were never seen in the dining room or hallways. Lilac continued the Bingo games; and the bridge club, book club and writer's forum met as usual, but those groups had never had an activities director around anyway.

Some slight changes were noticed. The little plastic honey servers that were always on the table ran out and were not replaced, causing some residents to complain that not only was the honey gone, the biscuits were smaller and dryer than usual. Linen napkins were replaced by paper ones. Granted, they were nice paper ones, but they were still paper. And some of the housekeeping staff and serving staff were no longer around.

"Strange things are happening," Robbie said one day at lunch.

"Speaking of strange things," Hadley said and pointed to the door. Thorny and Geoffrey were marching into the dining room. Geoffrey was moving around behind Thorny so he could get a good view of Mary Rose. When he did, he sat, stared at her, grinned a funny doggie grin and started to drool.

"Is it my perfume? Do I smell like a sirloin?" Mary Rose asked.

Marge smiled. "I had a perfume once that smelled like bourbon. It was a hit on the dance floor in college."

"Hello Everybody!" Thorny yelled. The Everybodies grew quiet and looked at him, some with squinty, suspicious looks. "I am pleased to announce," he said, patting Geoffrey's head, "that we will soon have fresh eggs and on occasion, a home-grown chicken."

"What about our honey!?" a man yelled.

"I don't know who your honey is, sir, but I do know about chickens. Because my sister, Rose, loves chickens, we have created an area for them to live, breed and lay eggs in one section of the property. I know you will enjoy watching them and will love the newly-laid eggs appearing on our breakfast buffet." Thorny grinned, touched Geoffrey's collar and walked out the door. Geoffrey was doing his best to walk by his master while still turning to see Mary Rose.

"Yuk," Mary Rose said, and she gave a little shiver.

Lunch was slightly cold thanks to Thorny's chicken announcement. Robbie and Marge both commented on how the salt and pepper shakers weren't full as they usually were, and Hadley poked a hole in her paper napkin. Just as they stood up to leave, things changed.

"Come here!" Wiley Vondra said loudly, rushing past them toward the big window, grabbing Mary Rose's wrist as he zoomed by. Alphonso was right behind him on The Mean Machine and Alphonso was laughing. They all hurried to the window and looked at where Wiley was pointing.

Zed Zonker, cane waving, was power-limping at full speed toward one of the big oak trees that stood regally on the Meadow Lakes lawn. Running not far behind him, wings flapping, comb and tail high in the air, was a big red rooster. If it hadn't tried to leap over a small shrub to gain on Zed, the chicken would have caught him. Zonker, with impressive speed, made it to the tree and actually pulled and scrambled his way up to a large, low branch. He sat on the branch and waved his cane at the rooster, who was circling the tree and, from the opening and closing of his beak, was making it obvious that he was squawking at full volume. Zed's mouth was opening and closing as well. It looked as if he was squawking back at the chicken.

Wiley Vondra was laughing an evil, satisfied laugh. He didn't like Zed Zonker and Zed Zonker didn't like him.

"Zed Zonker's been treed by a chicken!" Wiley yelled.

By now, everyone still in the dining room had gathered at the window watching Zed and the terrorist chicken. Zonker looked up, saw the crowd watching him, lifted his cane with one hand and gave them the finger with the other.

The watchers applauded.

"It's embarrassing to be treed by a chicken," Mary Rose said.

Wiley grinned, "Yeah."

"It would make it difficult to reclaim your dignity," Robbie added.

"Yeah," Wiley said.

"I wouldn't want 'treed by a chicken' on my tombstone," Marge smiled.

"Yeah."

"I suppose I should go rescue him," Alphonso volunteered.

"Why?" Wiley asked.

"Don't you dare hurt that chicken, Alphonso Greatwood!" Mary Rose ordered.

"Yeah," Wiley said.

"Here," Marge said. She handed Alphonso her Red Cane and pointed to the third jewel from the top. "If the chicken comes for you, aim the end of the cane at it and press this." Alphonso hung the cane over the handlebars of The Mean Machine, made a tight turn and took off.

In just a few minutes they saw him coming out the big doors of the dining room, down the ramp, across the sidewalk and onto the green space where Zed Zonker and the rooster were still squawking at each other. Zed was hanging onto his branch with one hand and waving his cane at the chicken with the other. The big red chicken wasn't giving up.

Alphonso drove at full speed toward the bird, who saw the scooter, jumped, flapped harder and hopped backward, its wings still waving and looking dangerous. Everyone watched as Alphonso motioned to Zed, then to the bitch seat behind him. Zed was shaking his head. Alphonso was nodding and holding up his arms as if he was ready to catch Zed if he missed the seat.

Zed pointed to the chicken.

The chicken attacked The Mean Machine.

Alphonso aimed Marge's cane and pushed the jewel she had pointed out.

A dense cloud of smoke surrounded men, machine and chicken.

There was a communal gasp from the crowd watching from the window. Then, with a sound of triumph, The Mean Machine roared out of the smoke screen with Alphonso at the wheel and Zed Zonker behind him. Their arms were raised above their heads as if they were on a roller coaster. The rooster had disappeared.

"Zed Zonker. Treed by a chicken." Wiley smiled. "My life is complete. My life is worth living. This is indeed a wonderful day." And he put his arms around Mary Rose and gave her a squeeze.

"That chicken had better be okay," she said with determination in her voice.

The window crowd had stopped applauding and was moving toward the doors leading to their apartments, still talking and laughing. As the girls turned around, they nearly collided with Frieda Grossemouth. Frieda was a good-sized lady dressed in a red jogging suit with red sneakers. She was an avid and generous Red Hat lady, and drove a pink Cadillac that was always parked by the girls' Hummer and Marge's Smart Car. Since Marge's little vehicle had red polka dots and plastic eye lashes over the headlights, it always made Mary Rose think the Caddy and Hummer had given birth to the little Smart Car. She especially liked it when the polka dot Smart Car was parked between the two big machines. Mary Rose McGill was all about family. She had even taken a picture of the cars parked together on her smart phone and sent it to all her daughters. None of them had replied.

"Did you hear about Gertrude and Heathcliff Hosemoff?" Frieda asked, her eyes wide. Her glasses were parked on her white curls making her eyes look less big than usual.

"You know they're trying to die together," she went on. The girls nodded. They remembered the sweet old couple asking Marge to shoot them. "Well, Gertrude and Heathcliff went out and bought new bathing suits."

"I bet Gertrude's has a ruffle around the bottom," Hadley smiled.

"Right," Frieda nodded. "Heathcliff bought a Speedo because he wanted to look like Michael Phelps."

They all grinned huge grins. It was an image worth getting rid of as quickly as possible.

"So," Frieda said. "they put on their new bathing suits, got Gertrude's hairdryer – which is a really old one, by the way – and got in the hot tub by the Meadow Lakes swimming pool."

The grins vanished and the girls held their breath.

"They dropped the hairdryer into the hot tub and it didn't work, but Gertrude had to reach down to the bottom of the hot tub to retrieve the dryer, and the chemicals in the tub turned her hair green. She had to go get her hair fixed." Frieda had finished her story. "They asked me to ask Marge if she would 'do them in' for money." She looked at Marge, her eyebrows raised and a small smile twinkling in her eyes.

"Nope," Marge smiled. "Not gonna happen. You say dropping the hairdryer into the hot tub didn't do the job?"

"Didn't know they had to plug it in," Frieda shrugged, smiled, waved at them and left.

"Didn't know they had to plug it in," Robbie repeated.

The girls went to Hadley's apartment and watched another Nancy Drew movie. The afternoon flew by and they had just enough time before dinner to take a short walk around Meadow Lakes while avoiding the area that was now fenced off for the chickens.

"I have to go to the ladies room before we go," Mary Rose said as they neared the quiet, comfortable lobby.

"We'll wait here," Hadley said, plopping down in one of the big, comfortable chairs that made a conversation center at one end. Sun was streaming in the big windows and it looked like a beautiful day. Robbie and Marge sat down by Hadley and started a favorite conversation of Nebraskans; they talked about the weather. Just as they were deciding that the spring had been a lot warmer than usual, Mary Rose McGill came scurrying out of the bathroom, her hand over her mouth. She dived into a chair next to Robbie, put her head down and began to laugh, her shoulders shaking.

"Okay girlfriend, what's going on?" Marge asked.

Mary Rose looked up, tears of laughter in her eyes. "I laughed so hard tears ran down my leg." She took a deep breath and then hiccupped.

"Rose," she stammered. "Rose Busch, the sister who is our accountant now?" She pointed to the bathroom door.

"I was walking to the sink to wash my hands, and Rose came flying out of her stall, backward, her feet in the air and her butt on the floor. She was flat on her back and her black skirt flew up over her head. She started yelling, 'I'm blind! I'm blind. I hit my head and went blind.'" Mary Rose bent over again, then straightened up, eyes lit up with delight.

"I pulled her skirt down and said, 'Rose it's alright. Let me help you up.'"

"What did she do that made her fly out of the toilet stall?" Hadley asked, grinning like the Cheshire Cat.

"She said the flush handles on the toilets had germs because people hadn't washed their hands yet when they flushed so she said you should always flush with your *foot*."

"Flush with your foot?" they said together.

"How do you do that?" Robbie asked.

"It obviously ain't easy!" Mary Rose said. "The handle sprang back when she flushed with her foot and threw her out of the stall on her butt. And with her dress up over her eyes, I could see her underwear. She had on bright pink cotton drawers with little Minnie Mouses all over them." They all laughed now.

"What did you do, Mary Rose, you rescuer of people in distress?" Marge asked.

"I helped her up and said I liked her panties. She told me I could get a pair online."

It had been a very eventful day, full of joy and hope and laughter. It was time for a good walk.

Part Two

Chickens, A Dog and Secrets on the Third Floor

Nancy Drew: "I just know that any time I undertake a case, I'm apt to run into some kind of a trap."

Nancy Drew: "Read, read, read. That's all I can say."

Nancy Drew: (*found a bomb in her car*) "Excuse me, I have to defuse this bomb."

Inga: "Oh totally. Love is a battlefield."

Robinson Leary: *Nancy had to be an avid reader. She talks bookish.*

Mary Rose McGill: *She had so many exclamation points!*

Hadley Joy Morris-Whitfield: *Could you defuse a bomb in your car, Marge?*

Marge Aaron: *I have a Smart Car. A bomb won't fit in my car.*

Wiley Vondra: *I think the Hardy Boys did better work, myself.*

Alphonso Greatwood: *Who the hell are you all talking about?*

Cold Food and Dust Bunnies

"Just look at this!" Hadley was standing by the big dining room window looking out at the Meadow Lakes lawn, frowning and pointing. Robbie, Marge and Mary Rose got up from table 12 and walked over.

"It's all gone to weed," Hadley said. "It looks awful and it was so beautiful before those dumb chickens took over."

"Are you talking about the birds or the Busches?" Marge asked.

"Yes!" Hadley said.

"That means she's talking about both," Mary Rose translated.

Hadley was right. In just a few weeks, the spring rains and sunshine had helped turn the area that had been fenced off for Rose Busch's chickens into a giant weed patch. The chickens themselves were pretty. There were the big red rooster, white and brownish hens and, it was true, there really were fresh eggs for breakfast one or two days a week.

"I like the eggs," Mary Rose said, "but you know what? The food in general is not nearly as good as it used to be."

"There's a new chef," Marge added. "Little guy. Looks like a weasel."

"The buffets are nearly always cold now, too," Robbie said.

"And what happened to the weekly Friday happy hour?" Wiley Vondra sauntered up behind them, a toothpick between his lips. "I liked those happy hours, and now Alphonso and I have to go to The Crypt for a cold one after a hard day's work on Friday."

Mary Rose gave him a friendly slap on the arm. "Yeah. Hard day's work." She grinned.

Alphonso Greatwood drove his Mean Machine up beside Marge. "It's after lunch. It's Friday." He looked at Marge then the other girls. "Let's all go to The Crypt and talk this over."

"I'm not sure what we're talking over, but a cold beer sounds really good right now." Marge smiled. "Can I ride in the bitch seat?"

Alphonso patted the seat behind his and Marge climbed on. The wheels of the scooter sank low in resignation.

"Count me in," Hadley said. "A glass of wine will let me stop whining about weeds."

"I'll do a Diet Coke," Robbie said and turned around to lead the way toward the front lobby.

"I can't go, but I want to point something out," a voice said from the doorway. A tall, thin woman in jeans and an Iowa Hawkeye sweatshirt was walking toward them. Ayneeda Coffee had dyed brown hair and thick glasses. Her sneakers squeaked as she crossed the floor.

"I heard you talking about the food and the weeds," Ayeneeda said. "I agree, and as you walk toward the lobby, take a close look at the carpet. It's dirty and all along the walls are dust bunnies."

"Dust bunnies!" Robbie exclaimed. "Dust bunnies are made up of lint and skin and clumps of dust."

"I didn't need to hear that skin part," Mary Rose said.

"Well, it's not all bad," Ayneeda Coffee smiled. "You can always joke about anything in life. What do dust bunnies use to fry their food?'

They looked at her.

"Dust pans," Ayneeda said and she gave them a friendly wave and walked past them through the dining room and out the door near the chicken yard.

"I've got one, too," Wiley grinned. "If you have a bunny with a hypodermic needle on its head, what famous song is it?"

They looked at Wiley like they had looked at Ayneeda Coffee.

"Furry with a syringe on top!"

They groaned and headed for the front door.

On the other side of the big apartment building, Geoffrey the Mastiff was playing fetch the stick with Thorny. Thorny was wearing a blue jogging suit. Geoffrey was wearing a three-foot-long tree limb covered with dog drool. When Mary Rose McGill stepped out of the door on the opposite side, the big dog stopped in his tracks, turned his head and listened. He never dropped the tree limb.

While the little group was going out the front door heading toward La Viva Crypt, inside Meadow Lakes Lilac Busch was tapping her four-inch heels against the floor and making angry phone calls to beautiful women while her sister, Rose, appeared to be working on two sets of books, recording numbers as if her life depended on it. Who knows? Maybe it did.

And as for Huckleberry "Whacker" Busch, still in his sombrero and poncho, he was hiding behind a tree on the front lawn, carefully watching the strange parade headed toward the little neighborhood bar. Not even Marge Aaron saw his long shadow interrupt the sunshine on the sidewalk.

The Crypt

There's something about a beautiful girl on
a motorcycle that stops men's hearts. A large
retired homicide detective on a handicap
scooter gives an entirely different image.
Marge had her arms around Alphonso, her legs
stretched out and her glasses secured on top
of her head as they went down the walk to La
Viva Crypt a block away. Her Red Cane was
casually draped over one arm. When Alphonso
hit a bump, the tires on the scooter – which
were flattened more than ever now due to the
two heavyweight passengers – gave The Mean
Machine a hard bounce. The Red Cane slipped.
Marge grabbed for it, accidently pressing one of
the jewels as her hand went around it.

"Marge!" Robbie yelled.

"For Pete's sake!" Hadley said loudly and
danced her way off the sidewalk.

"Dear God in Heaven!" Mary Rose yelled
as her feet flew out from under her and she
landed flat on her butt. "Ouch!"

Alphonso braked to a stop and turned the scooter around.

Wiley was helping Mary Rose up.

Dozens of little tripping pellets were scattered all over the sidewalk, happily released from the third jewel on the Red Cane.

"Oops," Marge said, an embarrassed smile creeping across her face, "Didn't mean to. Now we have to pick all these little suckers up. I don't have refills anymore."

While La Viva Crypt was only a bar serving pub food and drinks, it was a cozy, warm, strange little place. Owned by Morgan Graves, the funeral director who also owned Billow DeGround Mortuary and Crematory, its décor reflected Morgan's work and his hobby: Day of the Dead.

In old Mexico, Day of the Dead is a fun and glorious holiday both celebrating the lives of those who have died while celebrating life itself. The main characters on this special day are skeletons: skeleton figurines, skeleton candy and skeleton costumes. Fortunately, most of the skeletons are smiling and happy. All of Morgan Grave's skeletons were ecstatic. And life-size. They were made of sturdy plastic and they weren't cheap.

The happy bone people were all around the place. Two of them, dressed as a grizzly bride and groom, complete with veil, bouquet and top hat, welcomed customers on either side of the front door. Two more in Mexican soldiers' uniforms guarded the side door. Others simply stood against the wall wearing colorful costumes and grinning at friends seated at the round tables. One skeleton was seated at the corner of the bar, outfitted in one of Morgan Grave's funeral director suits. He had a bottle of beer and a glass in front of him. No one had ever seen him pour and drink it.

The walls were covered with colorful paintings of Day of the Dead, and colors on the walls themselves were bright and cheery. In some ways, while good old Morgan was of British ancestry; his bar took you right into the heart of all things good south of the border.

And the bar itself was something else. It came from one of the old Omaha hotel lounges, The Lazy Leopard, which had featured live music and dancing along with good food and was located in the New Tower Inn at the 72nd and Dodge area. The motel had been hit by a tornado in the 1970s and what was left had been torn down years ago for a shopping area. But Morgan had attended the Leopard auction and come away with the best tables and chairs and the massive bar with beautiful carvings and elegant mirrors. He estimated it to be well over one hundred years old.

Moezy Liam, who stood behind the bar, was less than one hundred years old. Moezy, whose real name was Modesty, tended bar and was Morgan's younger but long-time girlfriend. She helped out at the funeral home by being an expert make-up artist for those most in need – the dead. Today she had bright red hair, long red nails and wore a red skirt with a long-sleeved yellow top. Her sandals had little jewels all across the top and could easily have spelled, "Walmart."

"Yo," was her standard greeting and she delivered it with a smile as the group pulled up chairs and sat down. Alphonso climbed off The Mean Machine and actually helped Marge disentangle herself from the bitch seat. He sat beside her at the table.

"Hey, Moezy," Wiley said. "I think you remember the girls." He pointed. "Hadley, Marge, Robbie and my lady, Mary Rose."

They smiled and nodded at Moezy, who smiled back and said, "Yo," again.

Their wines, beers and Diet Coke came right away along with Digger, Moezy's Great Dane, who quietly laid down beside Hadley, his head on his big paws. Wiley ordered Slabs and Bones for them to share. That meant burgers and fries in Crypt talk and also meant a tail wag from Digger who recognized that food was coming.

The other evidence of Morgan Grave's day job was a burial vault, the top of which held a Happy Hour buffet. Two old-fashioned wooden coffins, painted black, served as drink tables for a conversation area that also included couches.

"Are you the detective the Hosemoffs asked to off them?" Moezy asked Marge when she put the burgers on the table. Marge did an eye roll and nodded.

"You know the Hosemoffs?" Hadley asked.

"I know a lot of the folks from Meadow Lakes," Moezy answered. "They were in here just the other day on the way to get Gertrude's hair fixed."

"Hair fixed?" Robbie asked. She liked Moezy.

"Yeah. Since you won't do the honors," she said, grinning at Marge, "they decided to gas themselves. They put pillows down in front of the stove 'cause their knees ache and they didn't want to kneel on the hard floor.' Then they knelt down and stuck their heads into the oven. Turned that sucker on full blast. Didn't do the job."

The girls looked at each other. Mary Rose's eyes were wide. "Electric oven!" they said all together.

"Yep," Moezy nodded. "But it did a number on Gertrude's hair. Limp as a wet noodle. She had to get a new perm." Moezy trotted off to her post behind the bar.

"Electric oven," Wiley said, smiling. "Every apartment has an electric oven. Hard to gas yourself in an electric oven. Lucky Gertrude's hair didn't go up in flames." He shook his head and sipped his beer.

"So what is going on at Meadow Lakes?" Robbie was leaning forward on the table, her Diet Coke between her hands. "And I'm interested in something else. Twice I've overhead Rose or Lilac say something about being sure not to tell their mother. Mary Rose has heard it, too." Mary Rose nodded.

"Strange things are going on for sure," Hadley said and she began to count on her fingers, "Weeds, food's bad, everything is running out – like the honey and now there are no condiments on the table, you have to ask for ketchup." She took a breath. "The place is dirty, the new owners aren't friendly at all and they're doing some kind of extensive remodeling on my floor. I hear pounding and drilling, but only when I wake up at night. They don't seem to be doing anything in the daytime." She looked at Robbie. "What's a mother not to like?"

"And who are the nieces?" Mary Rose asked.

They all looked at her. "Nieces?" Marge asked.

"Yes. They must be nieces because they're very young, they dress like the young girls do, in mini-skirts and short tops and they wear heels and have tattoos and big hair. They wear a lot of leather skirts and shorts."

"They wear leather." Wiley said, smiling. "Men must like them. They smell like trucks."

"How do you know they're nieces?" Marge asked after she did an eye roll.

Mary Rose turned toward Marge, "Well, they must be. I've seen one with Zed Zonker and one with that new man, Colon Oskomee. Each time the guys met them together at the door, and then they left right away, like they were taking their nieces out to dinner."

The table was totally silent.
"Now that you mention it," Wiley said.
"Zonker has been real happy lately."

Marge grinned. "He probably has a very nice niece."

Hadley leaned forward. "They're running a prostitution ring!" she whispered.

"Bingo, girlfriend," Marge said.

"How did I miss that?" Alphonso asked.

"Prostitutes!" Mary Rose whispered loudly.

"They've been in here for drinks." Moezy appeared at the table. "Anybody need anything else?"

They ordered another round.

"And something's up on the third floor," Marge said.

"Should I call the sheriff?" Hadley asked. The sheriff was her attractive Native American relationship, retired sheriff Wes Longbow.

"Not yet," Marge said. "Let's look around ourselves first."

"This is so Nancy Drew!" Mary Rose grinned and almost clapped her hands.

That's when Marge happened to look up and began to squint at one of the skeletons standing next to the two guarding the side door. This one stood still as a statue and was wearing a poncho and sombrero and seemed to have a handlebar mustache. She squinted harder, blinked and the skeleton was gone. "Huckleberry Busch," she said under her breath.

The Third Floor

Early the next morning, Hadley hurried out of her third floor luxury apartment and headed to the elevator just across from her apartment. She got there the same time as Beulah Bachaus and Adah Ashcroft. Both women were pulling big suitcases on wheels behind them and had hangers of clothes over their left arms.

"Where are you two headed?" Hadley smiled. Beulah and Adah were busybodies and generally a pain in the rear, but they were quiet neighbors and each had a small studio apartment alongside Hadley's big one. The three residences made up the entire wing of the big third floor.

"We're moving, Hadley," Adah answered.

"Moving? Really."

"Yes. Mr. Thorny Busch gave us such a deal." Adah's voice was consistently soft. "We get to move to one bedrooms on the second floor."

"For the same price as the studios," Beulah added.

"Really." Hadley said again, getting more and more curious. "What a great deal. Good for you. How did you pull that off?"

Adah smiled. "We didn't. Mr. Thorny Busch just called us to his office and offered it. He said they were going to turn our apartments and the conversation room between them into a larger convention-meeting area. Have you heard all the pounding and drilling going on?"

"I have. I have indeed," Hadley said. Then all three got into the elevator. The last thing Hadley saw when she looked toward the end of the hall was two large men with moving dollies taking chairs and a couch out of one of the studios.

"So there's going to be one big room on the third floor," Marge said after Hadley told the other girls over breakfast.

"For meetings and conventions," Robbie said. There was skepticism written all over her face.

"What would Nancy Drew do?" Mary Rose asked.

"Go see what's going on!" Robbie answered.

They sat quiet for awhile. Hadley went to the coffee bar and brought back a pot of decaf and poured it.

"You didn't need to bother," Robbie said, taking a sip. "It's cold."

Mary Rose was thoughtful.

"You know I go to Bingo now and then, and every so often if I sit by Lilac Busch, and her phone rings, and she talks to someone, well, a lot of the time I hear her say, 'Don't tell mother.' What do you make of that?"

"I'd say there's something they don't want their mother to know," Hadley said.

"Mary Rose," Marge went into her cop voice. "When's the next Bingo game?"

"Actually, it's this afternoon at three."

"Let's slip up to Hadley's and take a look at the third floor." Marge was leaning in with her arms flat in front of her on the table. The dishes were stacked in one corner, waiting to be picked up after a mediocre breakfast. There were no fresh eggs today. "Then Mary Rose, you go to Lilac's office a little early, ask if you can help her with anything setting up Bingo, and ask about her mother."

"Yes!" Mary Rose said, her eyes twinkling. "I love doing cop things!" She put her hand into the air over the table and three others high-fived her.

Throw the Stick!

"I can hear the pounding through this wall here," Hadley was pointing to a wall in her living room. "So they have to be working on this side."

"It's a long wing," Marge said. "That could go a heck of a way back."

"I'll go see if the workers are gone in the studios," Robbie said and she walked out Hadley's door and into the hall. In less than a minute she rushed back, eyes wide, slammed the door behind her and leaned against it, panting.

"That damn dog is out there!" she exclaimed. "Geoffrey is guarding the one studio. I just got in here in time."

Hadley went to the door, opened it a crack and peeked out. "He's there. Way down at the end of the hall by the studios."

"We need to get him into the elevator," Marge said. "Mary Rose, you need to draw him here. The elevator is just across the hall. He loves to fetch." She looked around. "I'll find something," and she started going through the rooms in Hadley's apartment. In just minutes she came back with a big piece of ornate white driftwood that was the main decoration in Hadley's bathroom.

"That's my driftwood from Florida!" Hadley exclaimed. "No way!"

"Way," Marge said. She handed the driftwood to Robbie and opened the door just a crack. "When I get into the elevator, Mary Rose, you stick your head out the door. When the dog runs toward you, Robbie will throw the stick into the elevator; I press the lobby button and run out."

"This is like that movie we watched, 'Night at the Museum,' where they had to throw the bone to get the dinosaur under control," Hadley said.

"Exactly," Marge agreed. "And that dog is as big as a small dinosaur."

Marge rushed out and punched the elevator button.

Geoffrey watched.

The elevator chimed and opened.

Geoffrey still watched, a line of drool coming out of his mouth and onto the carpet.

"OK, Mary Rose, draw him here," Marge said loudly.

Mary Rose stuck her head out the door and looked at the big dog at the end of the hall. "YooHoo, Geoffrey!" she yelled.

The Bull Mastiff rose up from where he was sitting, grinned an enormous grin and began to lope down the hall.

"Throw!" Marge yelled.

Mary Rose ducked back inside the apartment, Robbie threw the stick into the elevator and Geoffrey dived in after it without another look at Mary Rose. Marge pushed the lobby button inside the elevator and did a fancy dance step past Geoffrey, who had the beautiful driftwood secure in his teeth. The last thing Hadley saw before the doors closed was her driftwood from Florida being broken into little pieces and eaten by a monster dog.

Busted!

"You could have tasered him, Marge!"

They were walking as quickly as seasoned women can walk toward the studio apartments at the end of the hall.

"That was an expensive piece of driftwood, dammit!" Hadley was ticked and Marge didn't seem to care.

Marge turned her head to look at her friend. "Look at it this way, Hadley. Your driftwood probably saved Mary Rose's life. Besides, I don't taser dogs." She said the last words under her breath.

"What did you say?" Hadley asked, still irritated.

"I said I don't taser dogs." She thought for a second. "Their metabolism is different and it hurts more."

"So? That's bullshit!"

"That reminds me," Mary Rose said, panting heavily. "SHIT."

They all straightened up. It was their posture signal: Shoulders back, Head high, Eyes (I) straight ahead, Tummy tucked in. They all straightened up and tucked in their tummies, which only slowed them down a little.

The door to Adah's studio apartment was in front of them. Marge turned the knob.

Locked or stuck, one of the two.

She pushed.

Nothing.

"OK, stand back!" She raised her leg and kicked the door as hard as she could.

"Ouch! Oh crap! I forgot. That was my new knee. Oh man, that hurts."

"I'm sorry, I'm sorry, I'm sorry!" Hadley said, moving up and putting her arm around Marge's shoulder.

"Don't be sorry, sister, help me. We both run toward it and crash into it with our shoulders."

"You've got to be kidding!"

"I don't kid about stuck doors. On three. One... Two...Three!"

The two of them ran for the door and smashed into it with their shoulders. It loosened then swung open.

"That was easy," Marge said.

Hadley did an eye roll and rubbed her shoulder. "I'm probably going to need a new rotator cuff," she mumbled under her breath.
They went inside.

The little studio was empty except for some abandoned papers on the floor, a card table and what looked like an architect's drawing of a floor plan on the table. Robbie rolled it open and they looked.

"Wow!" Mary Rose said. "They are making one big area here."

"Look at this," Hadley pointed to a spot on the drawing. "They're putting in an elevator from the outside. You can get into this room without coming into Meadow Lakes at all."

"There are tables drawn all over inside the room," Robbie said. "Why would they need all these tables? Some rectangle, some round and here's a bar, I betcha."

They were quiet for a minute. "I've seen a place that looks like this somewhere," Marge said.

They stayed quiet while she thought.

"Gambling!" Marge had a strange smile on her face. "The S.O.B's are going to run a gambling den. And I bet they're going to do everything they can to get you to move, Hadley. You're the only one left in this wing and even with the elevator coming directly into the room, if you could hear them working you could hear voices and music if things get a little loud."

She put her hand on her chin and thought some more.

"Your apartment would make a really nice suite for the big gamblers and. . ." The wicked smile was back, "the nieces to do their jobs."

There was a voice behind them. "Well, well, what do you think, ladies?"

Thorny and Rose Busch were standing just inside the door. Geoffrey was on a short leash beside his master and already he was looking at Mary Rose and drooling.

Marge reached for her Red Cane and realized she'd left it leaning against the wall at Hadley's apartment. There was just a minute of silence, then Hadley broke out a huge smile and walked toward Thorny Busch.

"Thorny!" she said happily, "This is wonderful! We wondered what all the pounding and drilling had been about, so we came in to look. What a great idea to make this into a convention center. Think of all the possible new residents who will make good use of it."

She carefully put a hand on Thorny's shoulder while looking at Geoffrey who was looking at

Mary Rose. Hadley smiled more and continued. "When I saw those plans, I was thinking, what if I offered to move so you could have a big apartment to offer to conventioneers who needed to stay over. I've been thinking about a smaller unit since I really don't need three bedrooms. If you could give me a good deal on a two bedroom on the second floor, I'd be grateful."

The girls watched and listened, their eyes wide. "Doing his job for him," Marge whispered.

"And covering us really well," Robbie whispered back, a fake smile crossing her lips.

"So Nancy Drew!" Mary Rose whispered.

Thorny bought it.

"What a good idea," he smiled. "I'd never have thought of it. Rose and I came up here to check the work and were gifted with a fine plan. Thank you Ms. Morris-Whitfield. We'll talk about it before the week is out." He smiled and nodded.

The girls went out. Geoffrey and the two Busches went in.

"You're good!" Marge said as they walked down the hall.

"Yeah, well I need to go home and have a Diet Coke," Hadley said. "Come on in, girls, I need to breathe deep and drink something cold."

Bingo!

Mary Rose opened the door to Lilac Busch's office. A plaque on the wall outside read, "Activity Director." Inside, the office was a mess, with paper and boxes everywhere. Mary Rose smiled her best smile, "Hello, Lilac dear, may I sit down?" It was a good twenty minutes before three o'clock Bingo.

Lilac looked up from her desk and nodded.

"I was wondering if you wanted any help setting up for Bingo," Mary Rose asked, moving a loose, disarranged stack of papers from the only chair other than Lilac's uncomfortable looking one that held the new activity director's tiny hiney.

Mary Rose took a deep breath. "I know people don't realize how hard you work and how hard this job is, and since I have some time, I'll be happy to be your volunteer and set up Bingo for you."

Lilac looked at Mary Rose, her eyes squinting in suspicion. "You want to set up?"

"I know it's not hard dear, but it is time-consuming, and frankly," she took a tissue out of her pocket, wiped her nose and gave Lilac her most pitiful look, "I get very lonely sometimes, and I just knew if I stayed in my apartment I'd end up crying. I thought of the old saying, 'busy hands are happy hands,' and if I could help you my hands would be happy."

Lilac looked at Mary Rose and shrugged. "The Bingo stuff is over there." She pointed her head toward a cabinet in the corner. Mary Rose stayed where she was.

"You must get lonely too, Lilac. You're so much younger than your brothers and sister and there's no one else around here your age except the meal servers and workmen. And when your parents are both passed on…"

Lilac interrupted her. "What made you think my parents are dead?"

"Well," Mary Rose looked even more pitiful, "I would think since you work so hard here at Meadow Lakes and it's such a nice place for us seniors, your mother at least, if not your father, would want to come here and live close to you." She looked up and blinked.

Lilac looked back down at the paper she had been working on. "My mother's alive. She lives in Florida."

"Florida! Oh how fortunate. I know Florida. What part is she in?"

"Little town of Gotha, just outside of Orlando." Lilac wrote something on the paper and put it in a stack on her desk.

"And does she have a beautiful floral name like you and Rose?" Mary Rose leaned forward and almost batted her eyelashes.

Lilac laughed a bitter little laugh. "Hah! Her name is BeataRhonda. BeataRhonda Busch. She gave us all the crazy names." Lilac busied herself with a new sheet of paper.

"Has she remarried?" Mary Rose went into her innocent look and innocent voice. "If your father isn't around and if your mother looks anything like you, Lilac, there must be men after her all the time no matter how old she is."

Lilac actually smiled. "I'm afraid she looks more like Huckleberry." A somber look came over Lilac's face. "She's even mean like him." Then she caught herself. "Time to set up for Bingo Ms. McGill. Thank you for helping." She got up from her desk, went to the cupboard and loaded Mary Rose McGill down with everything needed for a serious Bingo game.

The First Date

"Gotha, near Orlando." Mary Rose McGill was proud of her detective work finding out where the Busch mother lived. The girls had met outside on one of the patios at Meadow Lakes because Marge had sent them all a text telling them to gather at the patio just before dinner.

"And her name is BeataRhonda. BeataRhonda Busch."

"Who thinks of these crazy names?" Robbie asked again, shaking her head.

Marge shook her head as well, then smiled at Mary Rose. "Very good." She patted Mary Rose on the shoulder then held out her hand, palm up. "Look at this." She was holding what looked like a tiny button.

"What is it?" Robbie asked.

"A bug. A hidden microphone. I found it under my coffee table in my apartment. I dropped my pen, it rolled under the coffee table and I saw it. I disabled it, and I'll reinstall it when I go back.

Mary Rose was excited. "Do you think I have one too?"

"I think we all have one. Ever since our run-in with Huckleberry his first day here, they've been suspicious. We'll look around when we go in. Heck, they may have one in every apartment, not just ours."

"Wow!" Mary Rose breathed.

"We need to wait till their operations are going full blast here, then we call the police and your sheriff, too, Hadley, if you want some time with the tall, dark and handsome one. Right now we got nothin'." She grinned, then went on. "I imagine they may know how to tap our computers and the phones in the apartments. We need to Google the Busch name in Gotha, Florida, and see who pops up, but we'll need to go to the public library and use their computers, or Hadley," she pointed her finger at Hadley, indicating she had just thought of this, "you can have Wes do it. He'd have better and more resources. He'd be able to find out a lot about the mysterious Mother Busch."

"Let me get this straight," Robbie said. "They're bugging our rooms, making a huge gambling area on the third floor and have at least two prostitutes working for them, right?"

"Right." Marge nodded. "They're probably laundering money and dealing drugs, too. Who would suspect an operation like that in apartments where old fogies live?"

"How would they launder money?" Mary Rose asked, looking excited.

"Easy. They'd run it through the rent books. Any kind of business can launder money, even a cleaners." She thought for a second. "A cleaners laundering money – I didn't mean it funny, but it was." She grinned, congratulating herself.

"They're very careful, aren't they," Hadley said. It wasn't a question.

Marge nodded. "They've done it before. But why all this 'Don't tell mother' stuff?"

Mary Rose answered. "They're Catholic. They have wonderful built-in guilt. Their mother doesn't know what they do and they don't want her to know. Big trouble if Momma finds out. 'Momma ain't happy, ain't nobody happy,'" she quoted.

They looked at her. Mary Rose shrugged. "I know this stuff. I actually dated a handsome guy in Catholic school. Every girl in the class wanted to be the one to convince him not to go into the priesthood." She had a far-away look in her eyes. "When he did become a priest, we called him 'Father Whatawaste.'" There was a pause. "We even dilly-dallied in the tall grass one day."

Robbie looked at Hadley. "Dilly-dallied in the tall grass?"

Hadley shrugged. "Every Catholic girl's delight, I guess."

They all got up to go in for dinner. "Casual talk at table 12," Marge ordered. "It's probably bugged, too. Tall grass talk is permitted."

As they sat down and smiled at the new server who sported a sleeve and neck of tattoos, a crew of workmen started installing security

cameras in every hallway and entrance of
Meadow Lakes Retirement Community.
Their casual talk at table 12 was more
interesting than any visiting about the Busches
and did not include grasses or landscaping of
any kind.

"I have a date," Marge announced as soon as
they had been served.

Their eyes opened wide and they all leaned in
toward her.

"Who?" Robbie asked with a big grin.

Marge paused then looked back at her.
"Alphonso," she said softly. "I'm sorry, Robbie,
I know you were his first choice and if you
don't want me to go, I won't."

They had never seen Marge Aaron so contrite
and humble.

Robbie laughed. "You go, girl! I'm all for it."

"Tell all," Hadley said, her grin matching
Robbie's. "Do tell all, girlfriend."

Mary Rose leaned in as close to Marge as she could get. "Yes, Marge. Where? When? How did he ask?"

Marge Aaron, retired homicide detective, actually blushed. "He called. We're spending the day together tomorrow starting with lunch at Mark's Bistro, then a matinee at the Orpheum Theater, then having drinks and dinner at Urban Wine Company."

"What will you wear?" Mary Rose asked.

"I have, believe it or not, a really nice black pantsuit, and also believe it or not, I'm as scared as a teenager on a first date." She looked off into space. "I haven't had a date in…," she paused then counted on her fingers, "eight years."

"This calls for something special," Hadley said. They were all grinning so wide they looked like a picture of monkeys at a banana party. She whipped out her cell phone and hit a speed dial number.

"Peyton, darling," she said when a voice answered. "Can you spare us an hour or more tomorrow morning? I have a friend who wants gorgeous hair and a makeover. Big date." There was a pause. "Nine? Perfect." She was quiet for a minute, then she smiled and said, "I know I owe you one, Peyton. I owe you a lot more than just one." She made kissing sounds into the phone, looked at Marge and they all did a thumbs up.

Peyton Claireborne

Peyton Claireborne was Omaha's most beautiful gay drag queen as well as a hair and makeup expert who had worked for several years in New York City with one of the big cosmetic firms. He had returned home to Omaha when his mother became sick and elderly and immediately opened a salon in the Old Market that looks like it had followed him home from New York. It is stylish, filled with huge vases of long-stemmed live flowers, the floor and ceiling are black, the walls hold huge mirrors or windows, the latter overlooking the big Missouri River. Peyton's stylists are always dressed in black, their chairs are black and Peyton himself was black. The salon is simply called "Peyton's" and it is as expensive as it looks.

"Oooh Kay," Marge said as she looked around. While the other girls had treated themselves to Peyton's scissors and nail polish, they had never brought Marge here. She was impressed and a little intimidated. "This isn't quite my style, ladies."

Marge looked good in her black pantsuit. She had dressed early in case her makeover and hairstyle took longer than she thought. She had on black two-inch heels and her whole outfit made her look almost trim. The Red Cane rested on her arm. It wasn't intimidated. In fact, it seemed to be enjoying the outing.

"Hadley!" Peyton Claireborne hurried toward the girls, hugged each and called them by name. Then he turned toward Marge, walked all the way around her, smiled and said, "Do-able. Yes, yes, quite doable."

"Peyton, honey, this is Marge Aaron, and she has a wonderful date with a very nice gentleman. We want to dazzle him and it's my treat."

Before she could argue with Hadley about who would pay, Peyton took Marge's hand and led her to his station. He sat her down in the chair, took some of her hair in his hands and said, "Here's what we'll do, my dear." Marge hadn't spoken a word. As the gorgeous black man talked into the mirror to Marge, two nail techs packed up their colors and equipment and began pulling stools over toward Marge.

A make-up expert, a young man named Andy, was putting together a pallet of colors while looking over his shoulder at the victim in the chair. Marge's Red Cane was dangling from a purse holder that jutted out from Peyton's station. It looked as if it was watching the whole thing with amusement.

"Wheatfield's for breakfast?" Hadley asked, and Robbie and Mary Rose turned on their heels, gave a little wave to Marge, who was sitting wide-eyed staring into the mirror while Peyton expounded and moved her hair around.

They walked up the street to the corner of 12th and Howard and the best breakfast spot in the Old Market.

"I move next week," Hadley said after their coffee was poured. "Thorny was so anxious to get me out of my apartment, he gave me an almost half-price deal on a two bedroom downstairs. It's not bad and since it's on the corner, it has a double balcony. I move free since I'm moving from one place to another in the building. They're painting it now and I went for some bright colors for a change; red, yellow, black and white."

"Sounds like Disney World," Robbie smiled.

"It will be great, Hadley," Mary Rose smiled and patted her friend's hand. "And if you put the TV in the right spot, we can sit on the balcony for our movie marathons. She grinned a big grin, "we can sneak up and watch what's going on up on the third floor." She took a bite of her cheese and ham omelet. "By the way, I saw the two nieces talking to Alphonso yesterday. Do you think I should tell Marge?"

Seasoned Women are Beautiful

"Geez," Mary Rose said as she looked at Marge. "You're beautiful, Marge. I feel like I should go home and dust myself."

"Beautiful," Hadley agreed, a big smile making her eyes twinkle.

"Absolutely gorgeous," Robbie chimed in.

Marge stood up from Peyton's chair. Her nails were a beautiful pink. "Strawberry Marguerite," she said holding her hands out for them to see. Her makeup was perfect, with a sculptured look on her cheekbones, dark and expertly applied eye shadow and lipstick a muted version of her nails. She looked great.

"We're not quite done," Peyton announced. "This is a tremendously distinguished lady. And only a few, even the most distinguished, can pull this off." He hurried into his back room and came out with a wide-brimmed hat that perfectly matched Marge's pantsuit. The red band actually matched the Red Cane and, if canes could talk, Marge's would be approving all over the place.

Peyton stood face-to-face with a new Marge Aaron, carefully put the hat on her head and arranged her hair even more carefully around it.

"Oh my God!" Robbie said, her hand going over her mouth.

"Jesus, Mary and Joseph!" Mary Rose exclaimed.

"We're making it sound like a religious experience," Hadley laughed.

"Maybe it is," Marge said. "Maybe it is."
She draped the Red Cane over her arm. The jewels sparkled in a match with her earrings. A beautiful, seasoned Marge Aaron broke into a huge smile and turned toward the girls, the two nail techs, Andy and Peyton. They all broke into smiles and applause.

"OK, you're beautiful," Robbie said from her back seat of the Hummer. She was squeezed into a corner while Marge sat almost in the middle of the seat, both her arms stretched straight out.

"I'm afraid I'll sweat," Marge said.

"Well with your arms straight out like that, you look like a giant blackbird ready to take flight." Everyone laughed except Marge, who didn't move her arms an inch.

Marge met Alphonso in the Meadow Lakes lobby at exactly 11:30. He came zooming off the elevator, dressed in an expensive Big Man Size suit, The Mean Machine polished until it glowed. His red tie was the same color as Marge's cane.

He turned down the hall, gunned his scooter, then looked up at Marge, who was actually posing, one foot in front of the other, standing at an angle, leaning seductively, both hands on her Red Cane.

Alphonso Greatwood came to a sudden stop.

He stared.

He grinned.

He drove slowly to Marge and held out his hand.

"Wow!" he said. He took her hand and hit the automatic door opener. They went hand-in-hand toward Alphonso's van, which had been washed and detailed the day before.

"Wow," Robbie said from the other side of the lobby where the three friends had been watching. "Wow," she repeated. "The man is a master of great pickup lines."

"Wow," Mary Rose and Hadley said together. "Wow."

The lovely couple didn't notice Huckleberry "Whacker" Busch peering at them over the hood of theHummer parked across the lot from Alphonso's big van. He had just secured a tracking device underneath the Hummer and now he stared at them as Alphonso opened the passenger door for Marge, opened the back of the van and loaded The Mean Machine and then himself into the vehicle. He stared at them as they drove out of Meadow Lakes' parking lot.

He was not wowed.

Here A Niece, There A Niece, Everywhere A Niece-Niece

"They should have been here half an hour ago!" Mary Rose McGill had been looking first at her wrist watch, then her smart phone for at least twenty minutes. Hadley and Robbie had both been secretly sneaking peeks at their watches as well. Neither of them responded to Mary Rose's exclamation.

Wiley Vondra pulled up a chair, turned it around so the back was toward the table and swung one leg over the seat and sat down, his arms folded on top of the chair back. "I used to be able to do that in one smooth move."

"We all used to have a lot of smooth moves, cowboy." Hadley laughed and gave his arm a friendly pat.

"I'm betting they spent the night together," Robbie predicted.

"They wouldn't do that on a first date," Mary Rose nearly whined. "They're old fashioned. They have old values." She hesitated. "They're old."

Wiley looked at her, then grinned.

"Bet you an ice cream at Ted and Wally's this afternoon," Robbie said.

"You're on!" Mary Rose said. "I'm saying they didn't sleep together."

"I'm with Robbie," Hadley said.

"Robbie," Wiley grinned. Mary Rose frowned at him. "Sorry." He didn't stop grinning though.

The dining room was full. It seemed the only people not finishing up their breakfasts and absent from the scene were the Busches, Marge and Alphonso. As the group at table 12 watched the door, two of the "nieces" walked through. They went through the breakfast line and headed toward the table next to the girls'. They both smiled at Wiley.

"Hi," they said.

"Hi," Wiley said back.

The girls looked from Wiley to the young women and back again. They were beautiful;

long hair, long legs, innocent-looking faces, painted nails and short, short skirts with tight, tight tops.

Hadley looked at everyone at table 12 then said, "Pull your chairs over here, girls. Let's get acquainted." They all looked at her.

"Okey Dokey," one of the girls said, and they both took plates in one hand and slid their chairs with the other. Mary Rose, Robbie and Wiley slid closer together to make room.

"We don't usually eat down here," the shorter one said, "it's rather nice."

Hadley smiled a soft, motherly smile. "We know how hard you work, girls." The others stared at her. Robbie's mouth fell open. "And you certainly deserve a good, healthy breakfast every day." Motherhood was oozing out of her pores now. She reached over and patted the hand of the young woman nearest her. "I'm Hadley. What are your names?"

The taller girl smiled. "Fonda Dix."

The shorter, pixie-like girl smiled as well, "Lovey Peters."

Mary Rose couldn't stand it. "Those are terrible names! You're both beautiful young girls. You should pick better names, even if you are…are…" She was stammering.

"Ladies of the night," Wiley finished for her. He smiled and patted Fonda on the shoulder. Both young women looked confused. It was obvious everyone at the table knew what they were doing at Meadow Lakes and everyone but the little blonde in red glasses seemed to like them.

"Oh," Fonda Dix said. "Those are our actual, real names. Our working names are Bambi Bam Bam and E.Z. Laye." She leaned in and smiled at Mary Rose, whose eyebrows were getting acquainted with her hair line.

"Hey Mary Rose," Wiley was still grinning. He hadn't taken his hand off Fonda's shoulder either. "Our generation had Pussy Galore and Octopussy for names."

"Those were *Bond* girls from 007 movies!" Mary Rose looked at Wiley as if that explained everything. She reached over and took his hand away from Fonda's very trim shoulder.

"Do you keep busy here?" Robbie asked.

"Not really," Lovey Peters replied. "Now it's almost like we're companions because the gentlemen here are so…." She looked at Wiley and smiled a guilty little smile.

"Ancient," he finished for her. She nodded. "But when Club Iwantitol on the third floor opens, we'll be busy. Then we'll both be able to finish nursing school."

"You've got to be kidding!" Robbie said.

The two girls looked confused. Robbie looked a little embarrassed. "I mean – companioning all these old gentlemen, what could be better than some nursing skills?"

"Oh. Yes," Fonda said. "But one of them is famous and he's very nice."

That was when Marge and Alphonso walked through the door and headed for the breakfast buffet. Marge was still wearing her black pantsuit with the jacket unbuttoned to show a somewhat mussed white blouse. Alphonso had on a comfortable Kansas City Chiefs jogging suit.

"Robbie wins!" Wiley said, almost yelling it.

"Not yet, she doesn't!" Mary Rose said, just as loud.

The two young girls looked at each other and shrugged.

"Ice cream bet," Hadley explained.

Marge and Alphonso headed toward table 12 and Wiley grabbed two more chairs from a table nearby that had just been vacated. Dirty dishes were stacked on top of it waiting to be picked up.

"You spent the night together!" Wiley said as soon as Alphonso had moved from scooter to chair.

He gave Wiley a high five. Marge looked flustered and embarrassed.

"Crap!" Mary Rose said and her hand immediately flew up to cover her mouth.

"Well," Marge said. "It was a very nice day." Her hair still looked great. She had told Peyton she really liked the style actress Judi Dench from the James Bond films had when she played "M" in the movies and Peyton had worked his magic. Marge actually looked a little like Judi Dench, just twenty pounds of more Dench than the real Judi.

"Have you heard about the Hosemoffs?" a voice from behind them said. Ayneeda Coffee came over and put both hands on Alphonso's shoulders.

"Don't tell us they actually pulled it off!" Marge said, reaching over and putting her hand on Alphonso's thigh. The big man seemed covered with hands.

"No, but this was a close one." Ayneeda looked at everyone at the table. Her eyes widened just slightly when they reached the young hookers. "They jumped off the Mormon Bridge."

"Jumped off the Mormon Bridge!" Robbie and Marge said together.

Ayneeda went on. "They put on their new bathing suits, got Zed Zonker to drive them to the bridge..."

"Idiot," Wiley interrupted.

"Then they stood on the edge of the bridge, their canes over their shoulders, cheeks together, arms around each other, eyes closed. And because their eyes were closed, they didn't see a river boat cruise ship with a huge swimming pool on the upper deck coming up the river."

The group at the table began to smile, even the young guests.

"They jumped, went into the pool and when they popped up, there were all these gray-haired ladies standing around the pool applauding. It was an AARP Widows Cruise, and when Heathcliff climbed out they started putting twenty dollar bills in his Speedo. Gertrude didn't get anything and she hasn't spoken to him for two days. She also had to get her hair fixed again." Ayneeda laughed and walked away, grabbing a slice of cold bacon on her way past the buffet.

Everyone at table 12 had pretty well finished eating by the time Ayneeda ended her story. Now one of the young girls looked up at

Alphonso. "Fonzie, how's it hangin' honey?"

Alphonso looked at Marge, a terrified stare in his eyes.

"You three know each other?" she asked.

"Oh Fonzie is our fave," Lovey said with a smile. "He's famous and he's rich."
Fonda nodded.

"You want to hang out after breakfast, Fonzie-Poo?" Lovey asked.

Marge stood up. "Oh for heaven's sake!" she said, then she turned and stomped out of the dining room. Her heels made a loud sound on the hardwood floor.

Fonzie-Poo pulled himself out of his chair and into The Mean Machine in record time. He almost did a wheelie as he burned rubber getting out of the dining room and following Marge down the hall.

"Fonzie-Poo has some 'splainin' to do," Wiley said, imitating Ricky Ricardo from "I Love Lucy."

When they looked around, Fonda and Lovey were headed out the door toward Zed Zonker who was waiting on the patio and Marge and Fonzie-Poo were long gone.

What Momma Don't Know!

"So you forgave the big lug?" Robbie was grinning at Marge as they walked around the Meadow Lakes lawn. All four were dressed in jogging suits that were either Nebraska Husker red or Creighton Bluejays blue. They were moving right along at a smart clip for old broads. Robbie and Marge were walking together, and right behind them came Mary Rose and Hadley.

"Life's too short," Marge said, puffing a little as the words came out. "He's a good man, he needs somebody now. He's never had a most important person and he likes me."

Robbie was quiet.

"And I like him, too." Marge smiled. "Plus, we spent the night cuddled up together, and I do believe those two 'nieces' when they say they're mostly companions to our old dudes here. Unless the Busches are trafficking in Viagra, we don't have to worry."

"Psssst!!" Mary Rose spit it out. "Look ahead." Her voice was a loud whisper.

Just ahead and to their right, sitting together on a park bench were Lilac and Rose, talking and gesturing to each other. A hedgerow of low bushes separated them from the foursome trying to power walk.

Marge held out her arms to stop them. "Crawl in behind those bushes and we can hear everything they say."

"If I point my good ear at them," Hadley whispered back.

All four friends ducked down, sneaked forward without making a sound and ended up side-by-side on their hands and knees, leaning their good ears almost into the bushes. It was a very Nancy Drew position. Lilac and Rose didn't hear them, couldn't see them and were talking loud enough for the sound to carry well beyond the hedge.

"But she would kill us if she knew what we were doing!" Lilac, the youngest sister was whining.

"I know, I know, dammit! Just leave me alone about it, Lilac. I have Momma convinced we're running a laundromat-carwash combo."
"Who does something dumb like that?" Lilac made a face.

"Hey – laundry is laundry. And we have a name, a fake incorporation file and everything. I know what I'm doing, baby sister. Just leave me alone and let me do it." Rose definitely had her big girl voice out.

"So what did you name it, Smartass?"

"Suds, Duds and Buds. We wash cars, launder clothes and sell beer. I even did some Photoshop work and sent a picture."

"If she knew we were running gambling, women and drugs, our asses would be grasses." Lilac bent her head and dropped it into her hands. It looked as if she was going to cry.

"Grow up!" Rose said. "No one's going to tell Momma." She stood up and walked straight ahead from the bench toward her chickens. Lilac hurried after her.

The girls looked at each other. "Drugs, too." Marge whispered. They were all still facing the bench on their hands and knees. No one moved.

"I hate to say this," Robbie whispered, "but I can't get up. I need something to hang onto to pull myself up." No one moved.

"Crap!" Mary Rose whispered. "I can't either."

Hadley just shrugged and tried to move one foot up to help her stand. "Forget it."

"So turn over on your butts and get up that way," Marge whispered.

"That doesn't help," Hadley said. "All that will do is get grass stains on our rears. We still need to grab ahold of something, Marge!" She whispered, too, and no one moved.

"I'll crawl over and put one hand on Robbie's back," Marge whispered back. "Then I can get up and help all of you."

"Why are we whispering?" a voice said from behind them. Whispering.

"Hey, Wiley!" Hadley smiled. "Give a girl a hand or two, will ya?"

Part Three

Testicles and Tempers

Personal ads seen in newspapers in Florida, the home of BeataRhonda Busch.

FOXY LADY:
Sexy, fashion-conscious blue-haired beauty, 80's, slim, 5'4' (used to be 5'6'), searching for sharp-looking, sharp-dressing companion. Matching white shoes and belt a plus.

LONG-TERM COMMITMENT:
Recent widow who has just buried fourth husband, and am looking for someone to round out a six-unit cemetery plot. Dizziness, fainting, shortness of breath not a problem.

SERENITY NOW:
I am into solitude, long walks, sunrises, the ocean, yoga and meditation. If you are the silent type, let's get together, take out our hearing aids and enjoy quiet times.

BEATLES OR STONES?

I still like to rock, still like to cruise in my Camaro on Saturday nights and still like to play the guitar. If you were a groovy chick, or are now a groovy hen, let's get together and listen to my eight-track tapes.

MEMORIES:

I can usually remember Monday through Thursday. If you can remember Friday, Saturday and Sunday, let's put our two heads together.

MINT CONDITION:

Male, 1932, high mileage, good condition, some hair, many new parts including hip, knee, cornea, valves. Isn't in running condition, but walks well. Can still drive at night.

DEVOUT CHRISTIAN:

Attractive lady wants to meet Christian gentleman who follows the rules.
Also must be able to remember the rules.

Accidents Happen

Hadley's furniture and belongings were being moved to her new apartment on the second floor. The pounding and drilling had stopped on the "conference center" on the third floor. The nieces came around now and then during meals and talked with the girls, Wiley and Alphonso. When they did, Alphonso moved close to Marge and kept quiet. They had taken other day trips and seemed to be getting along really well. Things had been quiet.

Hadley had called the sheriff about tracking down BeataRhonda Busch.

"Hi Wes," her voice was soft with a gentle roundness to it. "I've missed you, LawMan."

"Missed you, too, M'am." His deep voice wore a smile. Wes was tall, dignified and literally wore a white hat, a big Stetson that fit him well. He wore western suits, jeans and had a big Suburban with a sign that read, "Longbow Consulting. Call the Sheriff."

"We want you to find someone for us and find out everything you can about her," Hadley said.

"Her name is BeataRhonda Busch and she lives in Gotha in Florida."

"I'll be happy to do it, Hadley, but what's her real name?"

"BeataRhonda – like Beat A Rhonda Busch."

"Nobody has a name like that."

"Well, she does. And she has a son who's probably a hit man. I'm telling you, Wes, you won't believe what's going on here at Meadow Lakes." She filled him in.

"Christ on a cracker, woman! Stay out of that stuff. Tell Marge to call in her friends on the force, and I mean it!" Now he sounded like Nancy Drew's father!

"She says it's not time yet, Wes. We have to wait until they get the gambling hall on the third floor going and we're sure they're dealing drugs and laundering money." She thought for a minute. "I promise I'll be careful." Marge had assured her there was no listening device in her bedroom. She could say what she wanted, and she did.

Hadley leaned back against the headboard of her bed, curled her legs under her as far as she was able and settled in for a long, tender conversation with a retired sheriff more than a thousand miles away. He said something and she laughed a soft, tinkly laugh.

Call to an Omaha Sports Talk Program

"Hey – I want to comment on Coach Bo's spring training ideas. (pause) Whoa! Hey! There's a wreck right in front of me! This guy in a pickup crashed into a big old Hummer with four old ladies in it. Now he's walking toward the Hummer giving them the finger like it's their fault. Weird looking dude. Has on this crazy sombrero and poncho."

"Now the lady driver's rolling down her window. Whoa! She just tasered him! Ha! Ha! Ha! Oh man, now the old broads are all getting out of the Hummer. The guy is trying to get up and a tall lady is hitting him with an umbrella and stomping on his sombrero at the same time. Ha! Ha! Ha! Now the black lady is beating him on the back with her purse. Ha! Oh Geez, that purse is like a jackhammer – KaBam KaBam KaBam – and now this little blonde with red glass frames is hitting him on the head with a book. It looks like – yeah it is, it's a Bible! Oh man, she's bonking him with a Bible. It's a hardcover RSV and he's trying to get up. Ha! Ha! Ha! The big old driver is hammering him with a Red Cane. Ha! Ha! (gasps and coughs) He's on his hands and knees and trying to crawl backwards. Those old broads are still hammering him. Man. Oh Man! He's on his feet now, running toward his truck. Whoa! The Red Cane lady just shot a bunch of pellets at him. Man, he's dancin'! He's dancin' all over the street with those little balls under his feet. Whoa! He's on his butt. Oh this is too good! Now the ladies are just walkin' casually back to the Hummer. Everybody's out of their cars clapping for them. They're waving to the crowd. Oh, Man! The guy is out of here! He's burnin' rubber in the opposite direction. Oh, this is good!"

Round the Bend and Good Old Pine Grove

The Hummer's dented door had been fixed, Marge had had it washed, polished and detailed and had taken it to a friend, Danny Simpson, for a general check-up and oil change. Danny owned a former gas station at the intersection of Happy Hollow Blvd. and Country Club Ave. He gave good service, had moderate prices and hosted a Monday Night Football party for his regulars.

"I found it right under the right fender," Danny said, handing Marge the little tracking device.

She looked at it, turned it over in her hand and just said, "Well, well. Thanks, Danny." As soon as she got back to Meadow Lakes she parked the Hummer next to Thorny's Cadillac and casually planted the tracking device under the Escalade's fender. Then she dialed the other three girls and told them to meet her at the Hummer because they were headed for Ted and Wally's in the Old Market for ice cream. No one argued with her. They were beside the Hummer in record time.

"I think we need to get away from here for awhile," she told the girls when they had settled down in one of the small booths at Ted and Wally's. Hadley cradled her Sinful Chocolate, Mary Rose had chosen a Crazy Caramel, Robbie was already tasting her Rocky Road and Marge had a double dip of Cherry Berry in front of her. "These guys are nothing but trouble and I just need to get away from it all and think, think, think." She told them about Danny finding the tracker under their fender and how she had switched it to Thorny's SUV.

"Let's take the Hummer and trailer and do a staycation," Robbie grinned. "You know, where we get away but we stay in the area. I read about a campground between Omaha and Lincoln where we could set up for a week or so, see how things go here and then decide what to do. We can mess around in Omaha or hit the Hay Market district in Lincoln." She took a bite of her ice cream and beamed at them. They thought for a minute.

"Robinson Leary, you have good ideas," Hadley smiled.

"I'm in," Mary Rose said.

"I can be ready tomorrow," Marge added.
Robbie went back for seconds on the ice cream.

Check in at the Office!

Pine Grove RV Resort was nestled in a typical rural Nebraska setting. While a pine disease had destroyed a lot of the bigger pine trees, there were good, shady sites and an easy off, easy on from Interstate Highway 80 (I-80).

"Exit 420," Robbie said, just before their GPS told them to exit left. A truck stop loomed on their right with a number of eighteen-wheelers already parked for the night, even though it was only late afternoon.

"Oh yeah!" Hadley said. "This is the Greenwood exit. The Baker Candy Factory is here. OK girlfriends, I know one tourist attraction we're hitting for sure. That's the best candy ever."

Robbie steered the big Hummer and the trailer around the curves to a large sign that read, "Welcome. Pine Grove RV Resort. All vehicles must register at the office."

They went a few feet farther on the graveled driveway.

"All visitors must register at the office."

As they stopped at the office, a third sign read:

**"STOP HERE.
REGISTER AT THE OFFICE.
CAMPERS ONLY BEYOND THIS POINT."**

Mary Rose laughed. "I think they want us to register at the office." They climbed out of the Hummer and went inside.

The office was spacious and smelled of fresh cleaning solution. The front part was actually a lodge, with comfortable round booths, tables, happily growing green plants, a giant TV and a small campers' store. Continental breakfast was served every day and there were pizzas and other snacks available. Marge looked out the back door at a big, beautifully landscaped swimming pool.

"Nice place," she said.

"Well, hello," a voice said from a small office tucked into a corner area. "I didn't hear the bell when you came in. I'm Harriet. I was out mowing, then checking the oven."

Harriet was an attractive lady in her seventies. She was even more attractive because she was carrying a tray full of crème puffs hot and fresh from the oven. She grabbed a stack of napkins, walked toward the girls and held out the tray. "Have some," she smiled. They had some.

"These are fantastic, Harriet," Hadley said, taking a second bite. Marge went to the big cooler in the back of the store area and grabbed four sodas to wash down the crème puffs.

Harriet smiled, sat the tray down and tucked a stray strand of hair into the gray French twist on the back of her head. She turned toward the office and yelled, "Cathy! The bell isn't working!"

Before they could finish their crème puffs, Cathy, the campground owner was behind the registration counter. She was trim with a blonde ponytail and, like Harriet, was dressed in dirty jeans and a dirt-smudged T-shirt. They had obviously been working outside and working hard. Both women kept trying to control stray strands of hair that had been wind-blown out of ponytail and twist.

Cathy smiled, let them look over the available sites and registered them for the one they chose. They would be staying a week and would re-register if they decided to stay longer.

"I like it that you have people register at the office," Mary Rose said, almost laughing. "Makes us feel safe." She was never good at being sarcastic and that comment only came across as complimentary.

Cathy became serious, "Nobody gets in here without my knowing who they are and where they're going. We don't even allow delivery people in. You get a delivery, it's here in the office and whoever brought it has registered at the office." She nodded her head as if to say, "So there!"

Harriet leaned on the counter and smiled at them. "You girls here for the festival?"

"What festival is that?" Marge and Hadley asked, almost together.

Harriet and Cathy smiled broad smiles that made their eyes sparkle. "Why, the Testicle Festival, of course," Cathy said.

"Say what?" Robbie asked.

"The Testicle Festival at Round the Bend Steakhouse." Harriet's grin was even wider.

"A girl hasn't really lived until she's downed a plate of batter-fried testicles."

The girls looked at each other.

"You've got to be kidding," Robbie said.

"Wait a minute!" Marge broke in. "I've heard of that! The guys in homicide never missed it. This weekend must be Father's Day, right?" She looked at Cathy and Harriet.

"Right!" Harriet smiled again. "Testicle Festival every Father's Day weekend. Round the Bend is really close to here. Everybody in the campground goes. It's a riot. And if you're not into testicles, see if you can eat all of The Ritz, their big steak."

Mary Rose's eyes got wide. "I think Wiley and Alphonso would like that."

Hadley smiled. "So would the sheriff."

The sheriff said he would indeed like it and Hadley could meet him at the airport the next day. They decided to literally "get a room" at the Hotel Deco, a trendy getaway made up of suites and the best showers in Omaha and located in the Old Market. They would meet everyone at Round the Bend when the Testicle Festival began. They ate at the Jackson Street Tavern, strolled the petunia-covered sidewalks and bought Wes a new jacket at Overland Sheepskin. As they strolled slowly around the lake on the ConAgra campus, Hadley put her arm through Wes' and smiled at him. "Old age is coming at a really bad time," she said. "I wish we were ten years younger, Wes."

Wes patted her hand. "So we walk slower, sit longer, see less and hear very little. That's what people do, Had. They grow old and then they die." He was the only person other than her husband who had ever called her "Had." She liked it.

Hadley sighed. "I'm not ready to die. I like it here."

She slipped her hand off his arm and let it settle comfortably into his. They wrapped their fingers together. With the other hand Hadley pulled her sweater tighter as a cool June breeze blew across the lake and the fountain sprang into the air, sending a gentle mist over them. Then she let go of Wes' hand and put her arm around his waist. He held her close and they walked on – slowly.

It's Just A Lot of Bull

Round the Bend Steakhouse sat high on a hill just a few miles off I-80. Close by was the tiny town of South Bend, which boasted a sign on County Highway 66 that said, "South Bend. Next four exits." South Bend was four blocks long.

Wes' rental car pulled into the big gravel parking lot at exactly the same time as Wiley Vondra's pickup truck. Right behind Wiley was the Hummer. All three vehicles lined up side-by-side. They didn't notice the fourth car, a small, nondescript sedan that blended in with the other cars and parked between two big pickups near the exit.

"Party Time!" Wiley yelled as he shook Wes' hand then gave him a manly hug. Robbie and Mary Rose gave Wes a kiss and hug each, and Marge added a high-five and an arm slap to her hug. "It's the 'coply' thing to do," she explained. One cop to another.

The sun, low down in the west, was casting long shadows from the trees in the valley below. The wind blew hard on the hill, but the steakhouse was so huge it didn't seem to matter. The big wooden structure had a comfortable, sizeable bar, and a big wooden-floored dining room with high-backed booths that kept conversation quiet and private. The long white tables in the booths were $29.95 at Target. Two walls held big windows, and a massive shelf high on the other two walls held antiques and historic items such as old washing machines, copper boilers and various farm equipment. It was Nebraska country through and through. Most of the booths and all of the tables in the center of the dining area were full. Laughter filled the space and live music was coming from the huge area just past the dining room.

"It looks like a convention center back there," Marge said as a smiling server with Lisa on her name tag led them to a booth near a window. The booth could hold eight easily. "Lisa will be your server," Patty May said as she handed them menus.

"We'll have one more, but he'll need to sit here at the end of the booth," Wiley told Lisa. "He's on a scooter." He turned to Hadley and Wes.

"Alphonso's coming in a few minutes. He had some business to take care of or I'd have ridden in his van with him." He looked around at his dining companions. "Nice site you have at Pine Grove, but I had to register at the office."

"Everybody has to register at the office," Mary Rose said. "You could be dangerous," and she gave him a peck on the cheek. His Stetson was hung on a hook on the outside of the booth along with Marge's Red Cane.

Their drinks arrived in just minutes and a pleasant Lisa went over the menu. It didn't get any better than at The Bend. The Ritz Steak was big enough for two or more, burgers, hot dogs, trout, all kinds of sandwiches.

"This looks good," Wes said, reading the menu item by item.

"You should come for our Friday night all-you-can-eat fish fry," Lisa said. "But come early."

"I'm getting us all T-shirts," Hadley laughed.

The servers were wearing colorful Testicle Festival tees and a lot of diners were wearing them as well. Some were obviously from years past. "And of course we start off," Hadley added, "with TESTICLES!" She looked up at Lisa. "Will three appetizers of fried testicles be about right for us?"

Lisa smiled, nodded and noticed Mary Rose crinkling her nose. She patted Mary Rose's shoulder. "Be ready to be surprised. They're good."

They were. In fact, they were so good that they didn't notice the nondescript man from the nondescript car sitting at the bar in the other room, on a stool at the end where he could watch the action at their booth. Huckleberry Busch was wearing a Nebraska Cornhuskers Blackshirts T-shirt and a red Huskers hat. He had shaved his handlebar mustache and beard. Even with so many in Testicle Festival T-shirts, he fit right in. Nondescript to the max.

"Beer, soft drinks, tea and testicles," Wes said.

"Life is good."

"They really are good," Mary Rose admitted.

"They taste kind of like breaded mushrooms," Robbie added.

"Balls are balls are balls," Marge added.

Wiley raised his glass. "Here's to the bull who sacrificed."

A cheer and a round of applause came from the doorway into the dining room. Alphonso Greatwood had arrived, and he was hungry and recognized. By the time he reached their table, he had signed four autographs for a table of gray-haired men in cowboy boots and testicle tees.

"It's Rocky Mountain Oyster Day," he said as he moved his scooter against the wall, grabbed a vacant chair, sat it at the end of the booth and eased into it.

"That's another name for fried testicles," Wiley told Mary Rose. She nodded and did an eye roll.

"Yo, Wes," Alphonso smiled.

Wes nodded. "FonzMan." They nodded to each other and Alphonso patted Marge's knee. She had carefully taken her place at the end of the booth closest to where Alphonso would be. She never was a dumb cop. The Fonz smiled at her. "We've got to get ourselves a couple of these T-shirts," he said.

The food was delicious. "A real cholesterol fix,"

Robbie called it. Alphonso actually ordered The Ritz Steak. "We ordered wrong!" Wiley said when he saw it. "Wes and I should have gone with that." But when their trout and pork chops came, they were happy campers.

TJ, the young second generation owner of Round the Bend, stopped by their table to say hello and have a menu autographed by Alphonso. "Don't miss the dancing and the adult tryke races," he said. And in answer to Robbie's questions, he told them how many of the antiques on the big shelves belonged to his family. He shook all their hands before moving on to the next booth.

"Testicles and adult tryke races," Marge said.

"You can mow 'em down with your scooter, Fonz."

Trykes and Grownups are a
Very Good Mix

The trykes were really go-carts without motors.
People peddled and laughed and bumped each
other around the huge indoor track in the back
of the steakhouse. Alphonso could barely fit
into one, but he and the other two boys gave
it a try while the girls sat at a table with decaf
coffee.

"I'm stuffed!" Robbie said.

"I'm full, too," Marge added, "but I'm going to
dance with Alphonso even if he has to stay in
his scooter.

He didn't. When the dancing started, Alphonso
and Marge danced a slow dance. Alphonso
leaned on Marge, a little heavily, but she didn't
mind a bit. Hadley and Wes, Mary Rose and
Wiley headed for the dance floor to join Marge
and Alphonso. Robbie sat with her coffee for
just a few minutes, then a handsome younger
man came over and offered her his hand.

"I'm Scott – from the campground." He had a
winning smile. "I'm Cathy's husband and I'd be

honored if you'd dance with me." Robbie saw Cathy across the room, she was holding a beer and waving at Robbie. Robbie danced.

Alphonso and Marge were dancing by simply moving back and forth, cheek to cheek. They looked like a perfect fit. The Red Cane hanging over Marge's arm had perfect rhythm.

TJ had described the weekend as a "let loose" time and it was. They had partied later than any of them, except Alphonso, had done in years. Wes was catching an early flight back to the coast, so he was staying with Alphonso for the night. There were hugs and kisses and goodbyes as they left Round the Bend.

No one noticed the nondescript man in the equally nondescript car follow the big Hummer out of the lot. Huckleberry "Whacker" Busch hadn't enjoyed the evening at all and it was way past his bedtime. He was in a very black mood. He fondled the handgun on the seat behind him and mumbled to himself as he drove with one hand on the wheel and left the long drive to the steakhouse exit. He didn't turn his lights on until the Hummer turned onto I-80 and he turned on right behind it. He had seen Robinson Leary get in the driver's seat. As long as the stupid old cop wasn't driving, no one would think about being followed.

Register at the Office!

The girls hurried into their jammies and housecoats, "I'm way too wide awake to go to bed," Hadley said. "Who wants a Caffeine-Free Diet Coke or decaf coffee?" All three answered in the affirmative. Hadley put on the coffee pot. The campground was just off I-80 and the song of the highway was loud with the trailer windows open. Down the road a Jake brake roared on an 18-wheeler and a siren sounded in the distance. Robbie thought how their BOOB Girl buddy, Maggie Patten, had loved the highway sound.

"It's not a full moon," Robbie smiled. "This month would be the full Strawberry Moon, but it's bright and I want to go out and see if we can see the stars. We're so far away from the city lights that the sky should be full of them." She opened the door and stepped out onto the first step leading down from the trailer. Immediately she jumped back in.

"I saw something!" She pointed to the corner of the campground laundry room. "I know I saw a man dart behind there. I could see him in the light on the laundry room and from those little lights on the posts by each site."

They gathered at the door and windows. Marge turned out the lights inside the trailer and reached for the Red Cane that hung on the back of the dining room chair.

They watched.

In just a few minutes they saw Huckleberry slip out from behind the laundry room. In the lights from the little building they could also see the gun in his hand.

"He looks better in his sombrero," Hadley noted.

"He's lurking," Robbie commented. "That's what I hate about the Busches; they tend to lurk."

"Who uses words like 'lurk'?" Mary Rose asked.

"Well they do," Robbie replied. "They tend to lurk."

"Lurking or not," Marge said, "I need to get him close enough to hit him with the cane's rifle."

"There's a rifle in there?" Mary Rose's eyes were wide and staring at the cane.

"I've never used it, but we still have a back-up taser if worse comes to worst."

They watched. Huckleberry was lurking his way to the trailer. Their heartbeats were speeding up as he got closer.

Just as Marge began to carefully push the door open enough to get the end of the Red Cane out, they saw Cathy driving up behind Huckleberry in the campground golf cart, lights off, totally unheard by any of them due to the highway noise. She stopped a short distance behind him, slipped silently out and, as he took another step closer to his goal, Cathy took a step to the back of the golf cart and pulled out a shovel.

As silently as any red fox in the cornfield beside the RV Park, she moved up behind Huckleberry, and with a stance and swing

Jackie Robinson, Robbie's namesake, would try to adapt and use himself, Cathy swung the shovel.

She hit the Whacker man flat on the back of his head. He went down. Her stance, swing and follow through were perfect. Even Tiger Woods would have been impressed with her swing. As the shovel came down from her swing, she gracefully stuck the business end into the ground and leaned on it like a pro.

The girls poured out of the trailer. Cathy stood in the moonlight, still leaning comfortably on the shovel. She grinned a wicked grin, tucked a loose strand of hair behind her ear and said, "He didn't register at the office."

Marge wasted no time. She pulled out a long piece of the golden lariat in the end of the cane's handle, pushed the jewel that released two nice-sized knives from the sides of the cane, cut the lariat and tied Huckleberry's hands behind him. He began to stir.

"Marge," Mary Rose said, "Let me taser him. Please! Please, Marge. I always wanted to do that."

Marge handed Mary Rose the cane, but before she let go entirely, she pointed to one of the jewels. "It's that one, Mary Rose. Aim carefully, girl."

Huckleberry was trying to turn over when Mary Rose pressed the jewel. They all were instantly covered with a thick, red, choking smoke.

"Not that one!" Marge yelled, fanning herself.

"Wait till the smoke clears and hope he's still there! Then press the jewel below that one!" In just seconds the wind had taken care of the smoke and Huckleberry was on his feet, staring at them and looking confused. Mary Rose aimed and pressed the jewel. The taser fired, Huckleberry's eyes got big as saucers, he put his knees together and went down.

"Wow," Cathy said. "Impressive crotch shot!"

"Very Nancy Drew," Robbie said.

"I'm calling the sheriff," Hadley said.

Wes Longbow, the sheriff, arrived with Alphonso and Wiley in Alphonso's van. They loaded a still unconscious Huckleberry Busch into the back, and after more hugs and kisses and a "My kind of womenfolk!" from Wes, a tip of the hat from Wiley and a big grin from Alphonso, they took off.

"I have some pretty good wine in the clubhouse lounge," Cathy said. They followed her down the gravel road between various dark, sleeping trailers, motorhomes and pop-ups, their house slippers making very little noise. The highway sang, the stars sparkled and the almost-Strawberry Moon shown down on them.

"We did what Nancy Drew would do," Mary Rose said.

"You did the most, dear," Hadley said. "That was a nice taser."

"I was thinking of my husband when I did it," Mary Rose said. She and Robbie were walking together just ahead of Hadley and Marge. "The last time I was at the cemetery I told him what I really thought. I said, 'We went through a lot together. Most of it was your fault.'"

Hadley looked at Marge. "We've been through a lot together. Most of it was your fault?"

Marge shrugged. "Works for me."

None of them seemed traumatized or especially upset that they had taken down a tough man who was coming after them with a gun. They hadn't grown old by being stupid. They had lived long enough to have seen the ups and downs, to have been on the roller coaster of life. They were widows and not much surprised them. They definitely had STDs – they were Strong, Tender, Determined and Smart.

"SHIT!" Robbie whispered loudly. They pulled back their Shoulders, held their Heads high, Eyes (I) straight ahead glancing down and Tummies tucked in. For old ladies walking in house slippers down a gravel road, they had remarkably good posture.

When they got to the campground lounge, they all sat in one of Cathy's big booths, their second big booth of the evening. Cathy brought out wine and glasses, and they talked and laughed as only women can. Hadley thought about

Mary Rose visiting the cemetery and realized they hadn't walked through the cemetery to their husbands' graves in a long time. And that was all right.

Part Four

If Mama Ain't Happy
Ain't Nobody Happy

Could these be Nancy Drew quotes?

*"I would travel to the ends of the earth
to solve a case."*

"At the very least, I'd go several miles."

*"I'm sorry, Ned. I really like you.
But a girl's best friends are her best friends."*

*"Sometimes the weather here is so hot
chickens lay hard-boiled eggs.
And squirrels pour cold Coke on their nuts."*

*"It's never too late to become
what you might have been."*

Meanwhile, Back at the Ranch

"So what do we do now, Oh Noble Leader?" Hadley was asking the question as she poured Marge a second cup of coffee. They were sitting around the little dining room table in the trailer, still in their housecoats. Even though they had not gotten to sleep until after midnight, they were all up before 8 a.m., sporting puffy eyes and bed head. Not one of them had brushed her teeth yet and they were still pumped from the night before.

"I've been thinking," Marge said, turning her cup in her hand, "We need to go back to Meadow Lakes, find out what's happening now and then…" She took a sip of coffee. "If things are going like I think they are, we need to go to Florida."

"Florida?" the other three said together, leaning toward Marge, their eyes widening just a little.

"If this goes like I think it will," Marge said, "the law won't be able to find any evidence of gambling, prostitution or anything else. Palms will have been greased and precautions taken.

There will be two sets of books and the old dudes with the nieces aren't going to talk to the police. A SWAT team could go in there and, when they got to the third floor, all the money would be put away and they'd be looking at a quiet game of cards between friends."

They looked at her. She smiled. "We need to go get Mama."

(BOOB) Girl Detectives

They had taken their showers, dressed and put on their makeup. Now they were outside at the picnic table, the morning sun warming their backs. "We all need to grab a few more clothes while we're at Meadow Lakes. Not many, just what you'll need to finish out a couple of weeks. Grab quick after you've done what you need to do."

She looked at Hadley. "Hadley, find out what the third floor looks like now. Take that new outside elevator if you can." She looked at all of them. "Today is Father's Day, if we go in around noon they'll all be at the annual Father's Day lunch. I read in the newsletter that one of the coaches from Creighton is there, so they'll have a big crowd."

"Hadley has the third floor. Mary Rose, get with Wiley and Alphonso, tell them where we're going and see if they've found out anything new."

She looked at Robbie. "Robbie, your job is to find one of the nieces. They liked you and they may tell you just what's going on. Offer them help on a scholarship to Clarkson's School of Nursing or something that will give them a way out of the profession and set 'em on the right track." Robbie nodded.

"What will you do, Marge?" Mary Rose asked.

"I plan to break into the offices while everyone's at lunch. Hand me my cane and let's go."

Hadley handed Marge the Red Cane and they went.

The parking lot at Meadow Lakes was nearly full. Robbie found a space by the side of the building where the Hummer was partly hidden by a large hedge. They got out and hurried into a side entrance.

"Good luck, girls," Marge said as they split up. Robbie wandered off down the hall toward the dining room to look for a niece, Hadley headed for the exit nearest the new outside elevator, and Mary Rose took the inside elevator to the second floor and Wiley's apartment, pulling out her smart phone as the doors closed in front of her. Marge and the Red Cane headed toward the offices. There were a lot of people around, getting ready for the Father's Day lunch, and the girls blended in well.

Hadley Joy Morris-Whitfield: Girl Detective

The elevator was installed and working, but so was the keypad that opened it. There was no way she was getting a lift to the third floor. She sat down on a bench near the walk that led to the elevator and waited. And waited. She realized she was glancing at her watch every minute or so. After nearly fifteen glances, a couple walked toward the elevator. They were well dressed and holding hands. Two women were following them, also well dressed, but not holding hands. Hadley pretended to be fixing her shoe; then, when they were nearly at the elevator door, she got up and walked over. She smiled at the two women. They smiled back. Friendly. Friendly. The elevator doors opened and they all got in.

"Have you been here before?" one of the women asked politely.

"No," Hadley smiled even wider. "This is my first time. I hear it's great fun."

"Oh it is!" the second woman said. "Last time I was here I won $300 and a whole box of Viagra."

The other women and the man laughed.

Hadley laughed, too. What a friendly girl. She followed them to the open doors that used to be studio apartments and a big conversation room. The massive room inside was decorated like an old-time saloon and dance hall, complete with stage and honky-tonk piano. There was music from the forties floating out over the tables that held all sorts of various games from roulette to poker. A hulk of a man was standing just inside the door behind a maître-d's desk. He had a shaved head and wore a tuxedo. He reminded Hadley of an ape trying to have a touch of class.

"Invitations, please," he said. His voice was one of supreme boredom. There was hair on his hands.

Hadley looked around, then gave him her best smile. "Oh for Pete's sake! I left my purse in the car. How stupid. I'll go get it." She rolled her eyes and smiled again, then she lowered her voice to a whisper and leaned toward him. "Plus, I have to go to the bathroom." She put her hand shyly over her mouth and hurried toward the door. "See you in a minute," she said and she gave him a little toodle-oo finger wave. He didn't toodle-oo back.

Hadley hurried down the hall toward her old third floor apartment. She stopped in front of the door and looked around. The hallway was empty. She tried the doorknob. It turned and the door slid silently open. Hadley slid silently inside and closed the door behind her.

The apartment had been changed into a sex paradise. There was a new hot tub, mirrors on the wall and ceiling, plush furniture and a round bed. Hadley's eyes opened wide and she let out a little gasp. It was all one huge bedroom now, and a weird one to say the least. She went to a door beside a huge floor-to-ceiling wall mirror, assuming the room would be a closet, and opened it. Inside was a table, a bar and one plush chair. The chair faced the mirror, which was a floor-to-ceiling one-way job. Someone could sit in the chair, have a very expensive drink and watch what was happening on the round bed. "Yuk!" Hadley said out loud.

Just then very sexy music filled the room. The door to the apartment opened and Hadley saw Thorton Busch stroll in with a very attractive, very thin young woman who had model quality coming out of her pores and implanted breasts coming out of her low-cut, super short dress.

Hadley jumped back against the wall, then realized she could see them but they couldn't see her. She stepped out to see better, but couldn't bring herself to go any closer to the big mirror.

"You work here, my dear," Thorny said. He showed her the entertainment center that took up an entire wall, changed the music to "Bolero" and lowered the lights.

Bolero! Hadley thought. *How tacky can you get?* She was shaking her head. Then Thorton turned the young woman around and kissed her passionately on the mouth. His hands roamed over her hips and breasts and she responded like the pro she obviously was. Just when Hadley was deciding whether she wanted to watch or keep her eyes closed, Thorny's cell phone rang.

"Damn!" he said. He was breathing hard. He answered the phone, looked at the girl, put his arm around her and led her out the door. Hadley breathed out a long sigh of relief. She counted to thirty, slowly, then left the closet and went to the door leading to the hall. She listened, her ear pressed against the door. Nothing. She opened it a crack and looked out. There was no one around. She hurried down the hall, opened the stairway door and took the stairs to the second floor and her new apartment. She knew exactly which clothes she wanted to take to Florida when they searched for Mama.

Mary Rose McGill: Girl Detective

Mary Rose found Wiley and Alphonso dressed in suits, ready for the Father's Day feast, which would be good since it was being catered. She put her finger over her mouth in the "shhhh" sign and directed them outside to Alphonso's patio in case his apartment was bugged. She told them they were going to Florida to find BeataRhonda Busch and bring her back – if she would come.

"Heck, she may not even be alive," Wiley said.

"Do you want us to meet you there?" Alphonso asked.

"Not unless we call begging and groveling," Mary Rose said. "It's kind of a girl thing, finding a mother and everything."

They didn't know much. There were, indeed, more nieces around now, but even though the girls liked Alphonso, they obviously had orders to leave him and Wiley alone and not talk to them.

"Associating with you is bad for our reputations," Wiley grinned. "As long as we pal around with you, we don't learn anything."

"We've been eating at the Crypt," Alphonso added. "Moezy doesn't know anything, either. Not many people coming down from Meadow Lakes anymore and none of the nieces are showing up now."

They talked for awhile, hugged goodbye and Mary Rose went back through Alphonso's big apartment without saying a word. All she had left to do was gather a few clothes in a shopping bag and go wait in the Hummer.

She was unlocking her apartment when she heard him pounding down the hall. She could hear his breath, his panting. She tried to hurry. The key wouldn't work! She was pushing on the door and wiggling the key. Then the door flew open and Mary Rose flew inside. She was too late. Geoffrey was so close she could feel his breath. She ran to the middle of the room, turned around and he flew at her. She was standing in front of a little love seat. His huge paws hit her chest, she fell onto the love seat and it tipped over on its back, taking dog and Mary Rose with it. Her red-rimmed glasses flew off and slid across the floor. She tried to get her hands over her face but couldn't. The last thought that went through her head as she looked into his big, open mouth and saw his sharp teeth was, *I'm dead.*

Robinson Leary: Girl Detective

Robbie looked everywhere for the nieces. The little prostitutes were nowhere to be found. She even went into the library. No one at all was there. She grabbed a couple of mysteries and left a note for Loretta Ripp saying she had borrowed them. The hallways were mainly deserted. Robbie had spent a lot of time. She had looked outside, checked the picnic tables and even looked in the ladies rooms on the first and second floors. Neither Fonda nor Lovey was in the workout room. They weren't in any of the conversation rooms. Almost everyone was in the dining room listening to the band that had been brought in. Robbie had peeked in and looked carefully, trying not to be spotted.

No nieces.

She finally gave up and headed for her apartment to grab some clothes for the Florida trip.

That's when she heard Gertrude Hosemoff screaming.

She ran to the Hosemoff's apartment. The door was open and Gertrude was standing just inside. "Get help! Get help!" she cried. Robbie rushed inside. Heathcliff was lying in the bed, a sheet over his lower body. What looked like a stick was poking up against the sheet. Robbie recognized it right away. Lucy, a retired nursing instructor who lived across the hall, rushed in. Right behind her was Ayneeda Coffee.

"Gertrude! What happened?" Lucy asked.

"We saw the ads on TV," Gertrude said between sobs and gasps. "All about how if you have a bad heart you shouldn't take Viagra. Well, we thought maybe we could sex ourselves to death. We haven't tried it in years, so we both took some of the pills they've been handing out here." She grabbed Robbie's hand.

"But look what happened! This started two hours ago!" She pointed to the stick poking the sheet.

Ayneeda Coffee leapt forward. She yanked the sheet off and they were looking at Heathcliff's skinny penis. "Oh, Sweet Jesus, thank you!" Ayneeda said, putting her hands together in a prayer position and looking at the ceiling.

"That was the last thing on my bucket list! I asked God to let me see a four-hour erection!"

They all looked at Ayneeda, then at Heathcliff's erection. It was not impressive.

"I don't think your prayers were answered, Ayneeda," Lucy said. She pointed.

The erection was going limp. Heathcliff pulled a pillow over his head and sighed.

"Well at least this didn't damage your hair, Gertrude," Lucy said. "What did the Viagra do to you, dear?"

Gertrude sighed as well. "I got very gassy. This just isn't working. I think we'll give up and let nature take its course. Maybe we'll just die together naturally." She thought for a minute. "Trying to kill ourselves was a nice hobby, though. It occupied our time and kept our brains active."

"Whatever floats your boat," Lucy said, patting Gertrude on the shoulder. "A girl has to do what a girl has to do."

Lucy hugged Gertrude, Robbie did the same and they left together.

"Whatever floats your boat or erects your tinker toys," Robbie smiled as she and Lucy closed the Hosemoff's door behind them.

"Like I said," Lucy smiled. "at least this time it didn't ruin her hair."

Robbie headed toward her apartment for a few clothes.

Marge Aaron: Actual Girl Detective (Retired)

The Meadow Lakes offices were all on the ground floor. They were roomy and had sliding doors leading to comfortable little patios. Marge hooked the Red Cane over her arm and walked up to the office of Thorton Busch, Executive Director of Meadow Lakes Retirement Community. She walked as if she were meant to be there and was expected. The door expected her all right. It was locked tight.

Marge looked around. There was no one in sight. Through the sliding glass doors she could see the office was empty. She slid open a little compartment on the Red Cane and took out tiny tools. It took her almost three minutes to get the lock picked and the door open. She was sure no one had seen her. She was wrong.

There were filing cabinets lining one wall, a laptop computer open on Thorny's desk, a television set, a couch and two end tables with lamps. Marge headed for the filing cabinets and tried each one until she found a locked one. She slid open the little compartment in the cane once more and took out her tools. It

was another three or four minutes before the
drawer came open.

"I'm rusty," she whispered to herself. She
began to look through the files inside. She
laid one entire file out on the floor and
photographed the contents with her smart
phone. She did the same thing with three
other files and, as she put the last one back in
its place, she heard the key in the door to the
hall begin to turn. She tried to get up, but she
had been on the floor so long her back and
legs were sore and stiff. "Crap!" she said. She
leaned on the cane and pulled herself up…
slowly. The door opened part way and she
heard Thorny talking to someone in the hall.

"No, it won't work!" he said. Marge eased
toward the sliding glass door. Thorny was
arguing with someone, but they were staying in
the hallway, not entering the office.

As she got to the sliding door she looked
outside and grinned. Alphonso's scooter, The
Mean Machine, was shooting across the lawn
at top speed. She hung the Red Cane over
her arm, stepped outside and closed the door
behind her. She could still hear Thorny's loud

voice as he opened the door to his office, his back still turned toward her. Alphonso drove up, braked the scooter and Marge got on the Bitch Seat as fast as she could. She wrapped her arms around the big man and they drove past the sliding glass door just as Thorny turned and moved toward his desk. He never looked up.

Alphonso drove to the Meadow Lakes garden and stopped in front of a bench. He helped Marge off the Bitch Seat and they sat down side by side on the decorative bench. She began to cry. He put his arm around her.

"I thought I was caught for sure and I couldn't get up fast enough and I was scared like I didn't used to get scared and if he had found me I don't know what I would have done. It's not like the old days, Fonz, when I could do anything and it was exciting and adventuresome. Now it's not. It's work." She leaned on Alphonso's shoulder. He didn't say anything; he just kept his arm around her and waited.

"We're going to Florida to find BeataRhonda and see if she can do anything." Marge pulled a tissue out of her pocket and wiped her tears and blew her nose.

"I know. I saw Mary Rose."

"We're hoping, since they're all so afraid of their mother, that she will come back with us and do something. What she can do, I don't know, but I think we really just want to get away from here for awhile and feel safe." She paused. "And clean. Dealing with crap like this is dirty work. I'd rather have a dead body I could talk to and find answers and catch a killer or two."

"You want me to kill Thorny so you'll feel better?" Alphonso was smiling. Marge smiled back.

"No thanks." Marge was smiling, too. "And thanks for the ride. How did you know I needed the scooter?"

"I could see you from my window. I saw you go in." He gave her knee a playful slap. "Took you long enough to get in! Then I saw a man in a black SUV drive up, Thorny came out to greet him and I figured he was headed for his office. I didn't know how close it would be. I was going to knock on the sliding door, signal you and drive you off. We were lucky."

"I'm the lucky one, large black dude." She leaned over and kissed him on the mouth. He returned the favor.

"Drive you to the Hummer?" he asked.

Marge nodded and climbed back on the Bitch Seat. Alphonso took the long way to the parking lot.

Marge totally forgot about getting extra clothes for the trip.

Hadley was secure in the Hummer, her shopping bag of clothes clutched on her lap.

Robbie was coming out of one side door of Meadow Lakes at exactly the same time as the Mean Machine rolled up with Alphonso and Marge.

"Where's Mary Rose?" Marge asked, glancing in the Hummer at Hadley.

Hadley shrugged.

"Did anybody see her?" Robbie asked.

"I did," Alphonso replied, "but it was awhile ago. She left to go back to her apartment."

"I've got a really bad feeling about this," Marge confessed. "We'll give her five minutes, then we go in."

"Five minutes!" Alphonso said. "I can go in now and no one will think anything about it." And he turned the Mean Machine around and headed for the front entrance that had an automatic door opener for wheelchairs, walkers and, of course, Mean Machines.

Time dragged. They looked at their watches. "Be patient," Robbie said. "Never pull on a tulip shoot."

Hadley glared at her. Marge did an eye roll. More time passed. More watch glancing. More pulling on imaginary tulip shoots.

Then the side door opened and Alphonso roared out on his scooter, Mary Rose in the Bitch Seat and Geoffrey loping along beside them.

"I don't believe this!" Hadley said.

"Holy Moly." Robbie was shaking her head.

"L.I.B." Marge smiled. It was her term for, "Well I'll Be."

Alphonso pulled up beside the Hummer and Mary Rose struggled her way off the Bitch Seat. Geoffrey was right beside her.

"It was my make-up!" Mary Rose explained.

"It must smell like dog food. He licked if all off my face better than my Ponds Cold Cream Cleanser." She patted the massive mastiff and smiled. Dog drool. She looked up at her friends in the Hummer who were staring wide-eyed at the dog and Mary Rose, who now had both arms around the big dog's big shoulders. More dog drool.

"Can we take him with us?" she asked. "I just love him and he says Thorny isn't good to him and smells terrible."

"Mary Rose McGill!" Marge said. "That would be dog-napping. Get your tiny hiney in here! We've got to get out of here right now."

Mary Rose kissed Geoffrey on the nose. He wagged his tail. She gave him one more hug. More dog drool. She got her tiny hiney into the Hummer. Geoffrey looked forlornly at Alphonso. More dog drool.

Never Take A Palm Tree for Granted

They left Pine Grove early. The sun had barely peeked over the eastern plains when all four girls worked together getting things in the trailer secured, slideouts brought in, the sewer hose put away, the water hose disconnected from the water source, the electric cord stored, wheel blocks removed and the Hummer backed into position for a hitch-up. Coffee mugs in hand, they waved goodbye to Cathy and Harriet, who gave them a thumbs-up and blew them a kiss.

It would take them three long or four short days to get from Omaha to Gotha, the little town in Florida that BeataRhonda Busch called home just outside of Orlando. They had grabbed a James Patterson audio mystery from the trailer and were involved in it, not making a sound; Robbie and Hadley were in the back seat leaning forward so they wouldn't miss a word, intent on the plot and the voice enticing their imaginations. Sometimes they put in a Willie Nelson CD and sang along every time Willie went "On the Road Again."

"Oh Damn!" Marge said the first day out. "Damn, damn, damn."

"What?!" Hadley and Mary Rose said together. The audio book was just getting to a good part.

"I forgot my clothes and I only have one clean outfit." She gave the steering wheel a loud whack. Marge was irritated.

"We'll find a Target or someplace in St. Joe. Worry not, girlfriend," Hadley said, patting Marge from her seat behind the big driver. Marge nodded and got back to listening.

St. Joseph, Missouri, was a medium-sized city between Omaha and Kansas City. Known as the starting point for the historic Pony Express, it had a nice-sized mall and a Target store. Marge pulled in, parking the Hummer and trailer near the end of the parking lot.

"I have to get a couple of bras, too. Don't let me forget," Marge said as they went in the big store doors.

"What size do you take?" Mary Rose asked.

Marge grinned. "42 long." They laughed. Shopping was fun. They hadn't shopped together since the Busches had taken over Meadow Lakes. Mary Rose found a lovely silver cross necklace; debated paying the price, then decided she was too old to regret what she didn't buy. The cashier cut the tags off and Mary Rose wore it out of the store.

Robbie picked up a bright yellow jacket perfect for cooler nights, which would probably not appear this time of year in Florida, but which looked fabulous against her dark skin and salt and pepper hair.

Hadley put in a new supply of knee-high hose and trouser socks. She thought of how seldom she wore full pantyhose anymore and remembered the days when she wore a garter belt before pantyhose were invented. She mentally thanked the person who created them as well as colored tights, for which she was also grateful.

And Marge? Three shopping bags later, she hurried to the Hummer where the other three were waiting. "Did you remember the bras?" Hadley asked.

Marge stopped, lifted the first bag and pawed through it.

"Yep!" she said. She grinned from ear to ear and lifted out a big bra that was bright red.

"Go Big Red!" Mary Rose and Robbie said together.

They headed down the Interstate, toward beautiful Kansas City. Robbie was at the wheel.

They wound their way through the south, stopping to lay in a supply of pecans and let Marge and Robbie have grits with every meal. They avoided Atlanta and New Orleans because of traffic, ate at Elsie's Café in a small town when they decided to get off the main highway for awhile and drove past Panama City, Florida, in a driving rain. Every afternoon they treated themselves to a slice of pie or ice cream. All along the trip, Mary Rose watched carefully for the first palm tree sighting and was delighted when they started appearing regularly. They sang. They had long talks. Each slept off and on, but fortunately never when she was driving.

They also talked about how much fun it would be to be full-time RVers and be able to pick up and leave anytime they wanted, go wherever they wished and be free of so many possessions, even though they had all downsized to move into Meadow Lakes. They talked about it. Then they fell silent with each woman dreaming her own dreams. Hadley thought how great it was, even at an advanced age, to be able to dream. She knew there had been a time, after their husbands died, when dreams had seemed to die.

Gotcha, Gotha!

They tried three different RV parks around Orlando and Gotha, which Hadley's navigator on her smart phone insisted on calling, "Gotcha." None were a fit for them, even though Robbie had spent an entire evening Googling park after park.

"They looked good on the internet," Robbie said after they left a messy RV resort that had sites so close together you actually could pass Grey Poupon Mustard back and forth without leaving your rig.

Toward late afternoon they came across Turkey Lake Park, a city park in southern Orlando. There was no picture or ad in their campground book. Robbie had not found it on Google. Mystery park. Hidden. Lucky, lucky find.

Turkey Lake was one of Florida's many big bodies of water. They checked in at the Gatehouse and the four park representatives there gave them such a warm welcome Hadley suggested they adopt them all. Robbie suggested they just bring them donuts instead.

As they drove through the park for nearly one mile to the RV campground, Mary Rose squeeled and began counting palm trees. There were Grey Palms, Queen Palms, palms that looked like bushes on steroids and massive giant live oak trees with multiple branches that reached their gigantic arms to the sky. There was a children's farm and Gopher Tortoises. And when they turned into the campground area, their site, number five, was spacious and beautiful and, you guessed it, had palm trees.

"Never take a palm tree for granted," Mary Rose said with a tender smile. "You don't find a lot of them in Nebraska." They set up in record time.

"Here's where I want to go for dinner," Robbie said, holding up a tourist's booklet she had picked up at the Gatehouse. "Bubbalou's Bodacious Bar-B-Que." The ad featured dancing pink pigs and boasted of the best pulled pork in Florida.

Before they left for Bubbalou's, which was just down the road from them, Hadley and Marge walked around the RV circle of thirty-six sites filled with pop-up trailers, motorhomes and fifth wheels, as well as regular trailers like theirs. At one site, Hadley pulled out her cell phone and dialed Robbie. "Come across the park to site 32," she said. Robbie could tell she was smiling. "We want you to meet Princess Confetti."

Robbie and Mary Rose walked past the laundry room to site 32. There, grazing peacefully, not a care in the world was a miniature horse. It was about the same size as Geoffrey the Mastiff.

It was sweet and beautiful. It was soft and wonderful. It was a full-time guide horse. "Her lady is blind," Hadley explained.

An attractive, middle-aged man came out from behind the trailer and smiled at them. "She's a great little horse, isn't she?" he said.

"Does she lie down in the back of your van when you drive?" Mary Rose asked, pointing to a large van parked in front of the trailer.

The man smiled. "Nope. She stands up between us and watches out the windshield."

They laughed. "Drivers coming toward you must think they're seeing things," Marge said. They shook hands with the gentleman and made their way back to the Hummer to drive down the road to get some great barbeque.

"There are so many beautiful palm trees here!" Mary Rose exclaimed. "So many!"

BeataRhonda Busch and Yellow Dogs

They found a good breakfast place called Peach Valley, shared omelets and told Siri in Hadley's smart phone to find BeataRhonda's address in Gotha. Robbie related the history of the little town as they drove. "Founded in 1879 by German immigrant H.A. Hempel, after whom the main street is named. Population nearly 2,000 and not much there. The bigger town of Windermere kind of takes over, it looks like. One well-known restaurant, a post office and I imagine if we looked hard enough we'd find some kind of school."

"I bet everyone in town knows BeataRhonda," Hadley mused.

The GPS took them past a huge Mormon Tabernacle, small lakes and big houses. Money. Lots of it. Little tasteful plantings in the middle of the streets turning them into mini boulevards. Then wilderness. For a couple of miles there were no houses, no businesses, nothing. Robbie pulled out a map and began double-checking. Then the robotic voice of Siri told them to turn right at the next street. They did. Still nothing. After at least three miles they came to a monstrous old Victorian house nearly hidden by equally monstrous live oak trees. Behind the house they could see a small lake.

Marge pulled the Hummer up a circular drive in front of the door. The porch had pillars, a swing and a few chairs. In general, the whole place had a dilapidated, rundown look. They stood side by side next to the Hummer and looked.

"Dang place looks haunted," Mary Rose said.

"Looks deserted," Robbie said.

Hadley shook her head. "Looks old."

Marge changed the Red Cane from her right arm to her left. "Looks like we should go inside."

The old steps creaked as they stepped onto the porch. The front door was open. Robbie knocked on the screen door. No answer. She knocked louder. She took hold of the screen door handle and opened the door.

"Hello!" she yelled. They stepped inside. The living room was furnished with antiques and furniture not-so-antique. It smelled old but not unpleasant. There was a big bouquet of fresh flowers on the round table just inside the door and country western music drifted through the room from somewhere unseen.

"Mrs. Busch!" Marge yelled. It made Mary Rose jump.

"Mrs. Busch!" Mary Rose echoed.

They waited. Nothing. Then Robbie saw something through the windows at the back of the house. She pointed out onto the little lake on the back of the property. "There's a child in a boat out there."

They went to a back door and stepped out. Sure enough, in a slow-moving motor boat was what looked like a nine or ten year old. Hadley spotted a pair of binoculars lying on a table between two chairs. She picked them up, focused them and found the child and boat.

"Hah!" she smiled and handed the binoculars to Marge.

Marge found the boat and chuckled. "We've found BeataRhonda," she said, handing the glasses to Mary Rose and Robbie.

In the boat, having a merry old time at a very slow speed, was a tiny woman with her hair done up in a bun on the top of her head. Sitting on the seat behind her was what looked like an equally old and very ugly medium-sized yellow dog.

"She's so tiny!" Robbie said.

"Like four feet nothing!" Mary Rose said, and she jumped up and down and yelled,

"Yooo Hooo!" at the top of her voice. They all followed suit, jumping up and down and yelling. The little old lady in the boat finally spotted them, hesitated, then turned the boat toward the house. She came in to a little dock – slowly. She climbed out of the boat – slowly. She reached into the boat and took out a black cane. Marge gripped the Red Cane just a little tighter. The old dog followed her out, even more slowly. Then the old woman, who looked truly ancient, started to walk toward the house and the girls – slowly. The dog stayed right beside her.

"Why does she look so familiar?" Mary Rose asked, looking through the binoculars. She handed them to Hadley, who watched the old lady meander toward them.

"Oh my God!" Hadley said.

"Does she look like Huckleberry?" Robbie smiled. "Handlebar mustache?"

"No." Hadley shook her head. "She looks exactly like Maxine in the greeting cards!" She handed the glasses to Robbie, who only said,

"Hah! The dog could be Maxine's ugly dog." After more than five minutes the little Maxine lady had nearly reached the porch. She stopped, looked at the girls and squinted. The bun on top of her head was a dirty gray, she wore a flower print housedress that was baggy and looked homemade, her sneakers were dirty and scuffed and her cane was Walmart brown. The dog just looked stupid.

"Don't git much company here," she said when she finally got close enough.

"Mrs. Busch?" Marge asked. "BeataRhonda Busch?"

Mrs. Busch nodded. The bun on top of her head wiggled just a little.

Marge pulled out her old detective's badge in its case. "We need to talk about your children, Ma'am. They need your help and so do we."

BeataRhonda Busch actually puckered up and spit into the grass. "Little bastards. What have they done now?" She put her cane on the bottom step and boosted herself up. "Come on, George," she said to the dog.

"George?" Robbie asked, looking at Hadley. Hadley grinned and shrugged. "It makes him George Busch."

George Busch lay down on the porch and started licking his private parts. BeataRhonda motioned to the chairs scattered around the porch. She didn't invite them in.

"Sit!" she said. George looked up at her, decided she didn't mean him, and continued to lick.

They pulled the chairs close together and sat. BeataRhonda hopped up into the back porch swing and began pumping back and forth – slowly. Her feet didn't quite touch the floor.

She glared at them. "So?"

Marge explained. Every so often one of the girls would interrupt to add something. The only time BeataRhonda came even close to a smile was when Mary Rose told about Geoffrey licking off her make-up. She listened. She nodded. Her eyes became slits every now and then.

"I kept my maiden name when it wasn't popular to do that," the old lady said, shaking her head. "Each of those children has a different father. It's the different father curse."

BeataRhonda looked at the small silver watch on her wrist. "You fly down here?'

Robbie answered. "No, we have a Hummer and a nice-sized trailer. We drove."

"Trailer!" BeataRhonda's eyes twinkled. "I used to live in an Airstream. You have those sliders that make it bigger?"

They nodded.

"Don't like 'em," BeataRhonda said. "It's lunch time. We'll go have lunch at The Dog, then we'll leave."

They looked at each other.

"Come on!" BeataRhonda barked. George jumped to his feet as fast as he could and followed her inside. He waddled and expelled some gas. "Good doggie. Come on!" she repeated.

They came on.

Yellow Dog Eats

It was a fantastic restaurant. Yellow Dog Eats
was in an old house that had once been a
country store. It looked as if it had escaped Key
West and moved north. There were colorful
banty roosters and hens in the parking lot in
front of the building and more in the yard next
door. A sign on the restaurant's front door
instructed "Hippies Use Back Door."

Inside were photos of dogs, an uneven floor
and tables where not one chair matched.

From the kitchen came smells no one could
resist. There were walls of wine, sauces and
more. Redneck wine glasses – mason jars
on candlesticks – were for sale and the girls
noticed that everyone drinking wine had a
Redneck glass and the pour was generous.

A large glass counter held various salads, and a
second glass counter had desserts to die for.

"You're buying," BeataRhonda announced.
Hadley pulled out her credit card. They
ordered at the counter. Marge had a sandwich
called "Hot Diggety Dog," Hadley went for

the "Kitty Cat Nap Salad," Robbie tried the "Black Hound" and Mary Rose appropriately ordered a turkey sandwich called "Holy Crap." BeataRhonda ordered the "Mexican Mutt" and a beer. The others had soft drinks or tea. Then, without a word, BeataRhonda led them through the restaurant and out the back door into a seating area that was shaded, walled and tended over by a beautiful black cat. It was extremely pleasant, friendly and warm, but when the cat spied BeataRhonda it hissed, jumped onto a concrete bench and clawed its way up one of the big trees shading the patio. It flattened itself on a branch and stared at the old woman and George with its eyes in little green slits.

"This is a fun place," Mary Rose said to BeataRhonda. "Do you come here often?"

"Every friggin' day," the old woman glared at her. "I'm too old to cook anymore and I like Fish."

"I like fish, too," Mary Rose smiled.

"Not fish, fish," BeataRhonda was still glaring.

"Fish is the name of the owner. Good boy.

Should have married my Lilac and kept her out of trouble."

Just then Fish, the owner and chef, came by. "Yo BeataRhonda," he said. He was tall, handsome and relaxed. He didn't stay and talk. He had talked to BeataRhonda before. He glanced at the girls, shook his head and gave them a sympathetic glance.

A loud speaker bellowed, "Hadley. Your food is ready, Hadley. Come and get it." They walked back inside and brought their lunch to the large stone table BeataRhonda had chosen.

They didn't say they would like to stay another day. They didn't ask any questions. Nobody questioned BeataRhonda Busch. They knew they would go back to the trailer, move it out and they also knew that George would probably be going with them. The ugly dog was older than dirt. Hadley could tell. BeataRhonda had loaded him in the Hummer, brought him to Yellow Dog Eats and now he was lying next to a tree with a small area of ground around it. George definitely looked older than the dirt. The black cat watched the dog from its perch in the big tree. The dog slept. He snored. He also expelled gas on a regular basis.

BeataRhonda scurried as best she could when they took her home. She gathered an ancient flannel nightgown, bunny slippers, denture cleaner and that was it. "Don't need to take any clothes. Not stayin'." she bellowed. Then she and George led the way to the Hummer.

"Doesn't George need his dog food?" Mary Rose asked, a little tremor in her voice.

"Doesn't eat dog food," was all BeataRhonda had to say.

She sat at the picnic table at their campsite, the sun beating down on her skinny frame. The girls worked at unhooking and hitching up, sweating in the Florida heat.

"What's she going to wear?" Robbie whispered to Hadley as they wound the water hose up and stored it away.

"I don't have a clue," Hadley said and she did an eye roll. "At least we don't have to worry about convincing her to come with us." George lay by BeataRhonda, watching with interest. When people came by walking dogs, he showed no interest and didn't move.

"I wonder how old she is," Mary Rose mused.

"Old enough to not worry about dying young anymore," Robbie answered.

Hadley took the first shift at the wheel. BeataRhonda helped George into the Hummer, laid her head back and went to sleep. George was on the seat beside her, sleeping along with her. They both snored and both expelled gas. Those were the only sounds for the entire afternoon. The girls were afraid to put in an audiotape or turn on the radio. They rode in silence. It was strange.

Just before dawn on the third day, they were jerked awake by the trailer moving. It moved, jerked, then stopped. They had stopped at a campground at a pull-through site and hadn't unhitched the Hummer. Now the Hummer was trying its best to resist leaving.

"What the…!" Marge yelled. She grabbed the Red Cane, jumped out of bed then out the door. The other girls were on their feet watching from the window and holding on to the countertop in case the Hummer moved again.

"BeataRhonda, get out of there!" Marge yelled. They could hear BeataRhonda yelling back. George was nowhere to be seen. The quilt on the couch that BeataRhonda was using for cover was folded neatly. More yelling. Marge was hitting the Hummer with her cane. BeataRhonda was yelling. Marge was standing her ground and opening the driver's side door. They saw her literally lift a squirming BeataRhonda Busch physically out of the Hummer. They saw George looking out the door behind her, watching the action.

He seemed to be grinning. Marge tucked BeataRhonda under her arm and carried her to just in front of the trailer door. BeataRhonda was flailing her arms trying to hit Marge, but she was pinned down over Marge's ample hip.

She was kicking so hard one of her bunny slippers flew off with the effort, but her skinny legs and feet couldn't get the job done.

Marge dumped her onto the picnic bench.

"You sit right here! Don't you dare move!" She stalked back to the Hummer and lifted George out. She carried him in front of BeataRhonda so the old lady could get a clear view of her dog. "You move and I cut off his tail!" George seemed to be enjoying it all. He was still grinning.

"She's strong!" Mary Rose said softly, looking at Marge.

"Definitely comes in handy," Hadley said.

Marge climbed up the steps and into the trailer.

"Hurry your asses up!" BeataRhonda yelled. Marge dumped George on the floor inside the door. Hadley turned, opened the refrigerator and gave him two slices of bread. He woofed them down and expelled gas.

"She figured out if we start now we can be in Omaha around six o'clock, but she had trouble waking us up, so she just planned to take off. But she's so short she couldn't reach the pedals and see over the steering wheel. She actually unhooked the water and electric, so skip your showers, let's get dressed and hurry our asses up. I want to be rid of her!"

"I don't think I want to grow up to be like her," Mary Rose said as she headed for her suitcase.

"Me neither!" Hadley said.

In less than ten minutes they were in the Hummer leaving the campground behind.

"I need coffee!" Marge said as they reached the highway. She pulled into the first truck stop and fueled the Hummer. Hadley went inside for coffee, BeataRhonda's tea and five big muffins. She remembered at the last minute to grab napkins.

All My Children Is Not A Soap Opera – Or Is It?

"She just wants them all in one place, Alphonso, we don't care how you do it, you're a creative guy. Tell them you have money to invest or something, just be sure all of them are there." Marge was talking into her smart phone. Mary Rose was driving, exceeding the speed limit by only ten miles or so. The sooner they were free of BeataRhonda the better. The Omaha skyline was in sight. Freedom was just minutes away.

They pulled into the Meadow Lakes parking lot, trailer and all. Mary Rose stopped just outside the circle drive that led to the front door. Marge was on her phone again with the Fonz. "Thorny's office," she announced. They hurried into Meadow Lakes and headed toward Thorny's office. BeataRhonda was walking between Hadley and Robbie and behind Marge. She was so short and skinny no one could even see her.

Thorny was behind his desk, standing and looking at some papers Alphonso had spread out before him. Lilac was on Thorny's left and Rose Busch on his right. They were all interested in what Alphonso was showing them. Huckleberry was nowhere to be seen. Everyone looked up when Marge pushed the door open and they marched in. "What's going on?" Thorny said, way too loudly. All four girls took a step away, revealing the little, feisty, mean-looking, unhappy and stubborn body of their mother. George looked at the three siblings, put his tail between his legs and hid behind Alphonso's Mean Machine, expelling gas twice on his way. He wasn't used to moving that fast.

Total silence.

Much staring.

Then BeataRhonda began to move – slowly – to behind the desk and behind her three children. They turned, also slowly to face her. Mary Rose was sure Lilac was trembling. Rose's head was bowed and Thorny had backed his butt right up against his desk. He wasn't going anywhere, though. BeataRhonda had them cornered; trapped. She raised her cane and smashed it down on the desk between the two daughters. A reasonably heavy paperweight jumped and slid sideways. Three pens rolled off onto the floor. George put his paws over his ears and expelled gas again.

"You idiots!" BeataRhonda yelled at the top of her voice. "You nincompoops! You brainless morons! You fools, fools, fools!" With each "fools" she looked at a different child. "You shameless brats! Stupid! Stupid! Stupid!" She made sure each child got a "stupid," too. "You jackasses! You blockheads! You boobs."

"Does she know we're the BOOB Girls?" Mary Rose whispered to Robbie.

"No, and don't tell her," Robbie whispered back.

BeataRhonda wasn't done. "You dolts! Dunces! Imbeciles! Jerks and ninnies!" She had to stop and take a breath. Then for the first time she looked around the office. "Where the hell is the stupidest of all?"

Thorny's voice was soft and contrite.

"Huckleberry is in jail."

BeataRhonda took another deep breath.

"You bad, bad children!" She yelled. "I am so ashamed of you. You are cheats and criminals and I have prison waiting for you!"

All three children reached around and put their palms face down behind them on Thorny's big desk.

"Do you have one of them guest suites they advertise in these miserable jails for the elderly?" She was staring at Thorny and her voice hadn't softened a bit. He nodded. "Good! You're putting me up in it tonight. I want dinner brought to me! I want one of them Omaha Steaks – a big one! – and corn on the cob and a bottle of good Boone Farm wine.

Then in the morning," she paused for effect and looked at each child, "we're going home! You're going to spend the rest of my life taking care of your helpless mother!" (Not true). "The house needs paint!" (True). "The porch needs fixing." (True). "I want a garden with fresh vegetables!" (Not true). "I want a new boat." (True). "I want a cook and a housekeeper and a yard man and that's all of you plus

Huckleberry." (True). Then BeataRhonda softened. "I want my four darlings with me until the end of my miserable days." (Definitely NOT true). A tear rolled down her cheek.

"Wow," Hadley whispered to Marge. "She's good."

Marge nodded.

BeataRhonda looked at Thorny. "You go bail your idiot brother out of jail. Tell him he's skipping bail to go home and live with Mama." She looked at her daughters. "Go pack, you no good sluts!"

The girls dashed out of the office, not even glancing at Hadley, Marge, Robbie and Mary Rose. Thorny looked at Alphonso, reached over and signed one of the papers the Fonz had laid on his desk. Then he walked toward the door.

Mary Rose took a step forward. "Thornton!" It was amazing how she could imitate BeataRhonda. "Leave Geoffrey here. He deserves better than you."

Thorny looked at her, squinted, shook his head and whistled. Geoffrey came bounding in from a side door and headed for Mary Rose, who had just time to get to a chair before the big mastiff crawled onto her lap.

It was so peaceful. A server took a huge steak to BeataRhonda's suite. There was a cold bottle of Boone Farm and three steaming cobs of corn on her tray. A separate carafe held tremendously strong coffee and there was a long-stemmed rose in a glass vase. When the server knocked on the door, BeataRhonda yelled, "Come!" He came.

When the girls knocked on her door to thank her for rescuing Meadow Lakes, she yelled, "Go away!" They went away.

Bye Bye Buschies

The next morning BeataRhonda Busch was in the dining room filling two plates from the buffet. They were loaded plates, at that. She came over, pulled up a chair, and sat at table 12 – uninvited. She spoke before the girls had opened their mouths.

"You'll take me to the airport, get me a flight to Orlando and George and I will go home."

"What about your children?" Hadley asked.

"What about 'em?" BeataRhonda said.

"They're long gone. Vamoosed. Outta here. We won't see 'em again and when I do it will be too soon. Now shut up. Let's eat."

They shut up.

They ate.

They assumed BeataRhonda's second plate was for George, who was probably snoozing and expelling gas in the guest suite.

They had taken the trailer to its storage place as soon as BeataRhonda was finished yelling at Thorny, Rose and Lilac and pounding her cane on Thorny's desk. Now all the children's cars were gone from the parking lot. Geoffrey was still asleep on Mary Rose's bed and Sally, The Dog Lady, was scheduled to come for his first training session that afternoon.

"I'm going to hug BeataRhonda when we get to the airport," Mary Rose said as they walked to the Hummer. "I want to see what she does."

What she did was stand stiff as a statue, sigh a frustrated sigh, shake her head and drag George's dog carrier onto the plane. Hadley had taken out her credit card once more and paid an enormous price to get George and BeataRhonda into first class seats. It had taken BeataRhonda exactly one minute to convince the agent that George was actually a service dog and could not be parted from her. Hadley hoped there was no one in first class who was allergic to dog farts.

The Busch children, Thorny, Rose, Lilac and Huckleberry, were nowhere to be found. The girls wondered what BeataRhonda would have done if they had actually shown up to go home with her.

"She would have run for her life," Hadley said.

"She would have grabbed your cane and shot them all," Mary Rose said, looking at Marge.

"She would have scared them off in some way," Robbie decided.

Marge nodded. "I could have shown her how to use the cane."

Riding the Long Freight Home

Summer had put on its best dress. The trees were lush around Meadow Lakes Retirement Community. The girls had spent time at The Bookworm. They had movie marathons. They did visit the cemetery again. They made plans to go to Fort Robinson in July. Then, one day at lunch, a box arrived for Marge. The state had hired a temporary staff until there could be an investigation into the gambling and Viagra dealing. The nieces had mysteriously disappeared and it had been quiet for weeks – until the box came.

"What is it, Marge?" Hadley asked. They were all wearing shorts and their Testicle Festival T-shirts. They planned on watching James Bond movies all afternoon.

"Talk about James Bond," Marge said, looking at the return address on the box. "It's from my brother in England." She took her table knife and cut open the box. When she lifted the top, she gasped, then she took out an envelope that lay on top of whatever was carefully packed inside. She read the note and sat down hard.

"It's from my brother," she said softly. "Rather it's from his solicitor. My brother, Myron, is dead." She read on silently. She looked up at her friends and smiled a sad smile. "While we got along, we didn't keep in touch. I haven't talked to him for…" She looked up and thought for a minute. "Years." She sighed. She began to unpack the box.

Inside was an entire case of tripping pellets, refills for the smoke screen in the cane, two new knives, bullets for the rifle and a new lariat. The only things that were not included were batteries for the taser.

"That's the Secret of the Red Cane," Marge said. "My brother really was with the Queen's Secret Service. He really was 'Q,' the Quartermaster who invented all the James Bond gadgets. He made the Red Cane for me when I became a homicide detective. It was the sweetest gift anyone ever gave me." She sat down, put a napkin to her face and cried. The Red Cane, leaning against her chair, was quiet just like her friends at table 12.

As a fine old British Duke said in a documentary done by Lord Snowdon, "The most difficult part of growing old is, by all means, the death of one's contemporaries." It doesn't matter whether the death is one of your most loved persons or someone to whom you haven't talked to for years; that death leaves a hole in your being. Some holes are bigger than others, but each one brings us closer to our own deaths. Every day we come closer to dying. We all hope it is quick and painless, that we just lie down, close our eyes and pass into whatever waits for us on the other side. It is never easy and we must hope to do it with STDs – strength, tenderness, determination and smarts.

Epilogue

Wiley Vondra was pouring wine at table 12. Everyone in the dining room had been told wine and a celebration would be following dinner. Some people had even enjoyed dressing up for it. The good cooks were back and the menu had included a delicious chicken casserole. There were no more chickens on the lawn. The weeds were gone as well.

"Where's Alphonso?" Marge asked. "He hasn't answered his phone all day. I'm getting worried." No one knew where he was, but Wiley had a clever little smile that had lasted all through dinner.

The girls had done some serious talking about going full-time RVing.

"We could get a truck and a fifth wheel," Hadley had said. "Our friends have a 40-footer that has a fireplace, double refrigerator, king-sized bed and a pull-out sofa as well as a lot of windows and an island kitchen."

"It has to be big enough for Geoffrey," Mary Rose said.

"How about those big new motorhomes?" Marge had asked. "We could pull the Hummer behind it. That would be damn impressive."

"It has to be big enough for Geoffrey," Mary Rose said.

Wiley just listened and grinned.

"Wiley, you and Alphonso could get a pop-up trailer and we could all go together." Mary Rose smiled her most fetching smile.

Wiley just listened and grinned.

"We could go to California for the winter and the sheriff could come play with us for months," Robbie said, giving Hadley a friendly slap on the arm. Hadley laughed.

Wiley looked at the door into the dining room, pulled out his chair and sat down, taking a good-sized drink from his wine glass. The county attorney was coming into the room, He was buttoning his suit coat as he approached the buffet where everyone could see and hear him. Wiley tapped on his glass with his knife and everyone became silent.

"Ladies and gentlemen, I'm your county attorney and I have an announcement. Our investigation is over. A search is on for all the Busch brothers and sisters who were definitely involved in criminal activity here. The good news is that none of you are under investigation. You are considered victims and when we find the Busches, you may be asked to testify in court."

He took a deep breath and looked around.

Silence.

"The further good news is that just prior to his disappearance, Thornton Busch sold this property."

Communal gasp.

"We find that sale to be valid and legal. With that finding, may I introduce the new owner of Meadow Lakes Retirement Community…"

There was a long pause. The attorney looked toward the door to the dining room, then spread his arms in welcome. "Alphonso Greatwood!"

Alphonso, dressed in a custom-made suit from Parsow's Fine Clothing, rode in on The Mean Machine. He did not speed. He did not rev his motor. He just stopped next to the county attorney and accepted with grace and poise the standing ovation from all the residents of Meadow Lakes Retirement Community. No one clapped harder than Marge Aaron.

Alphonso looked at her, smiled and blew a kiss in the direction of table 12.

Nancy Drew would have clapped her hands and thrown her hat into the air!

The Omaha BOOB Girl Tour

When four BOOB Girls came by to hear me speak at a senior center, they told me how they had gone on a fun day trip to places mentioned in the books; places where Hadley, Mary Rose, Robbie and Marge are likely to show up on any given day.

If you are coming from West Omaha, go to 105th and Pacific and turn south until you find the beautiful **Happy Hollow Country Club** where Hadley has taken the group in nearly every book. Unless it's lunch or dinner time, you can probably find Kelly or Jim to show you the library, the girls' favorite room. Dorothy, who had worked at "Happy" for many years died this year. The place won't be the same.

Go back to Pacific St. and turn right. Drive to 87th Street where you'll find **Countryside Village** and **The Bookworm** and **Village Grinder**. It's time for outstanding coffee at the Grinder and to browse through one of the few and the finest independently-owned bookstores.

Drive on east to 72nd Street and turn left. Now you're at the area where Morgan Graves furnished **La Viva Crypt from the Lazy Leopard Lounge auction.**

Keep driving north to 72nd and Maple. Turn left and you'll be at **Centering Corporation** at 7230 Maple Street. This is the grief resource center Joy and Dr. Marvin Johnson founded in 1977. Drive into the parking lot, come in and say hello and have a cup of coffee.

You'll leave Centering, turn right, then make a U-turn to head east again on Maple. Drive by or stop in **Jane's Health Market** and **Leo's Diner** in the village of Benson. This is where Gary the Vampire joined friends for a Zombie Walk in *Boob Girls IV.*

Keep on to 49th Street and turn right. At the corner of 49th and Happy Hollow, the house on your right – a lovely little English Tudor – belonged to Joy and Marv for more than 30 years. Keep driving and you'll be at the **Homy Inn** where the girls went for champagne on tap. As you drive across Happy Hollow, look to your right. At the end of the block, by what is lovingly called the traffic peanut, is **Dan**

Simpson's Auto Shop. Danny found the hidden tracker in the Hummer.

If it's near lunch time, turn right at the Homy In and go to the top of the hill to 50th Street. Turn left into the village of Dundee. Park where you can and walk to **Mark's Bistro,** the girls' favorite restaurant at 51st and Underwood. If the weather is nice, have lunch on the most beautiful patio in Omaha. May I suggest Mark's famous Mac and Cheese, and ask for Mark. He'll be happy to say hello, show you Joy and Marv's booth and the table where Warren Buffett met with Hillary Clinton.

After Mark's, head south on 50th Street until you come to West Center Street. Turn left on Center and drive by **Kubat Pharmacy**, one of the few remaining family-owned pharmacies and where the girls bought the bed pan for Mary Rose's bedpan hat in *BOOB Girls II*.

Continue East on Center Street and you'll come to the **Old Market.** Now you're on your own. Visit **Wheatfield's, Vivace's, The Jackson Street Tavern, M's** and of course, **Ted and Wally's Ice Cream.** Stand beside the new Hyatt Place Hotel and look up at the third floor of the **Mayfair Building** across 12th Street.

The apartment near the back by the fire escape was Joy and Marv's and Robbie's. You'll be standing where Esmeralda sang her sad song to Robbie then patted the beautiful horse in **BOOB Girls III.** Go into the **Passageway Mall** where Wes and Hadley had dinner and go smell the leather at Overland Sheepskin where Wes bought a jacket. Keep walking East and you'll come to the Con Agra campus and lake.

If it's a nice day and you want even more good walking, the pedestrian bridge across the wide Missouri is just a little ways north.

Enjoy a good glass of wine by turning right and walking to the **Urban Wine Company** at 10th and Jones. Then turn around and head west toward 15th and Harney and Hotel Deco.

On your way, you'll likely pass the **Orpheum Theater** which holds all the grandeur from its prime.

Now drive back on Center Street to 84th Street. Turn left on 84th and go to **Mangelsen's,** where you can find just about everything you need, including help making a bedpan hat.

Hit the Interstate by **Mangelsen's** and head west. Drive to the Springfield exit and head south to Louisville. There you'll visit **Coop de Ville**, on main street, the neatest little gift shop ever. Walk around the corner to the big white house and explore **Feathers**, the other gift shop decorated by Dr. Liz and her ladies.

Have one of Dr. Liz's Scotheroos and, like Robbie, buy a purse. It's sayings from the Coop bathroom that start this book when Mary Rose looks in the mirror. "I do declare, I love my hair." That bathroom is worth a trip to Louisville anytime.

Get back on the highway by Louisville and drive a short distance to the sign reading South Bend. It's on highway 66. If it's close to dinner time, head for **Round the Bend Steakhouse,** home of the Testicle Festival. Careful. Don't miss it, it's on your left and high on a hill.

After too much food at the Bend, go north until you get to I-80 again. Head west to exit 420. There is **Pine Grove RV Resort,** home of Marv and Joy and where the girls went on their Staycation. Come in! Have a cup of coffee with us. Be sure to register at the office.

Go on to **Baker's Candies** in Greenwood and shop, shop, shop at the factory store. The gift shop is chocolate heaven.

You can dedicate an entire day to the zoo, where Marge and Alphonso had a date. I'm sorry but there is no Meadow Lakes Retirement Community. I picture it as being between Creighton University at 25th and California and the Old Market. There's no Peyton's Hair Salon, either. I picture it in one of the big apartment buildings near the river in the Old Market.

I also imagine I've left out some places. If I have, remind me and I'll add the revised version to **_BOOBs VI_**. Happy travels, and the coffee pot is always on at Pine Grove.

Thank you!

Biggest thanks and a huge hug to my daughter, Janet Sieff, Executive Director of Centering Corporation, who has designed all the covers for this series, been my editor and did the layout and design for all the books but one and just look inside all five and you can tell which one I did. Janet's fiancé, Marc Roberts, for his proofreading. Her sister, Jenny Ritter, gets hugged at the same time for being my fave reader and wonderful supporter.

A new bookmark and porcelain cup to my friends at **The Bookworm** and **Village Grinder**, who promote my books, give me hugs and have the best bookstore-coffee shop in the country, bar none.

A heavy new dictionary to our friend, Tom Vondra, who is married to my VSBFF, Mary. I owe Tom a big thank you for wonderful names like Hosemoff and for the rabbit with a hypodermic on its head that stands for "furry with a syringe on top."

Tom can share the dictionary and look for new names with Rev. Dr. James Campbell, the only other person with a warped mind equal to mine and with Dr. Gary Vance who gave me great ideas and who, with another VSBFF, Louise Vance knows all about dilly dallying in the tall grass. Louise had proofed every BOOB Girl book in the series. Gary and Louise join us every year at Fort Robinson.

And what could we give TJ, the owner of Round the Bend Steakhouse but a big, steaming plate of batter-fried testicles. And yes, there really is a fantastic Testicle Festival every Father's Day weekend. Ya'll come!

Lucy Wood gets a glass of wine from La Viva Crypt for ideas and support and Connie Gleason gets a cup of really good tea for naming Ayneeda Coffee. I don't remember who came up with Fonda Dix, but thank you, too!

A bowl of good dog food to Sally Whitaker who really is Omaha's Dog Lady and who has trained every one of our Bernese Mt. Dogs and who will do really well with Geoffrey.

Lunch and a new pen to Julie Himbert, my good friend who did a master job of proofing and consulting on this book. Julie named our annual lunch with members of the SW Library Book Club The Joy Thing. If you do find a typo anywhere in these pages, please blame Julie.

A really good casserole to all of you who got a free book by sending recipes to our ***Cluck and Gobble Cook Book.*** A second helping and a big hug to Ben, Nick and Kelsey at Centering Corporation who ship the books, sell the books and help me in more ways than I can count.

Happy Birthday, Nancy Drew

It's appropriate we dedicate this book to all of us who grew up with Nancy Drew, because... Nancy Drew is 80 years old.

Nancy Drew herself is a Burned Out Old Broad Nancy's History: Edward Stratemeyer a publisher, hired writers to create Nancy Drew. First was Mildred Wirt Benson. The writers initially were paid $125 for each book and had to give up all rights to the work and to maintain confidentiality.

Benson and Harriet Adams (Stratemeyer's daughter) are often listted as the primary writers of Nancy Drew books under the pseudonym Carolyn Keene, but there were others who used the name and wrote Nancy stories. Even Stratemeyer's secretary got in on the act, creating some of Nancy's friends.

So while there wasn't a real Carolyn Keene, there was certainly a Nancy Spirt who enthralled nd delighted us all, gave us so many exclamation points (!) and which lives on even today on bookshelves, in stores and in our hearts.

> We are all,
> Nancy Drew, Girl Detective

And coming soon...

Mary "Rose"

Meet The B.O.O.B Boys

(Burned Out Old B@st@rds)

de Wolf, John, Marv and Mark

Calendar Girl, Joy Johnson

About the Author

Joy Johnson is 76 now. With her husband, Dr. Marvin Johnson she co-founded Centering Corporation, North America's oldest and largest bereavement resource center and Ted E. Bear Hollow, Omaha's center for grieving children. She is a nationally-known speaker and has written or edited over 100 books on grief, mostly for children.

Joy's husband, Marv died in 2014. This book is dedicated to him and is the only one he didn't get to read and enjoy. However, Joy's three children, Jim, Jenny and Janet, all live near her in Omaha as do her six grandchildren, Jessica Joy, Paris Jennifer, Alex, Emma, Gregory and Liesel. Barney the Bernese Mt Dog is too big for her retirement community and lives now with Janet and Ben from Centering Corporation. Joy is at home with and loves a fat tabby cat named Margaret Thatcher.

If you enjoy this book, you'll love and laugh with:

The Boob Girls:
The Burned Out Broads at Table 12

The Boob Girls II:
Lies, Spies and Cinnamon Roles

The Boob Girls III:
Sandhills and Shadows

The Boob Girls IV:
Murder at Meadow Lakes

The Boob Girls V:
The Secret of the Red Cane

The Boob Girls VI:
From the Eye of the Moose

The Boob Girls VII:
Ten Little Puritans

www.theboobgirls.com

Visit the girls and Joy Johnson at:

www.theboobgirls.com

www.welcometothe boobgirls.blogspot.com

Joy is an international speaker who has presented delightful *Boob Girl* programs across the country.

Ask her about speaking at your group. You can email Joy at joy.johnson@msn.com

Other grief resources available through

www.centering.org

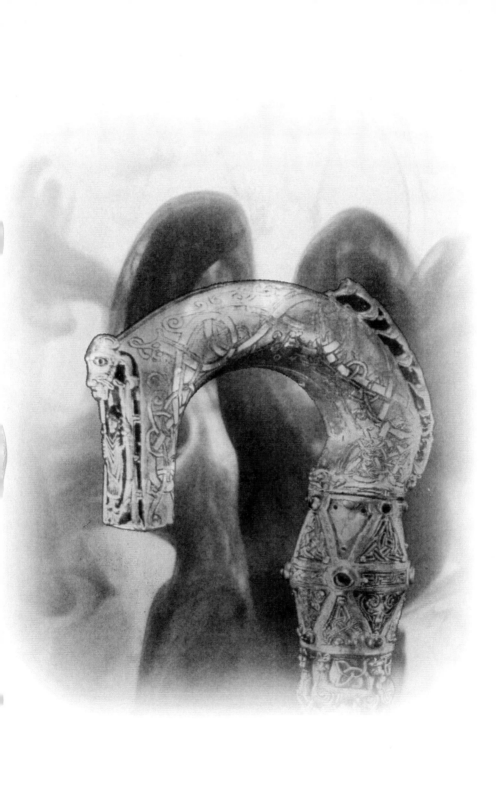

www.theboobgirls.com